CHECKING IT TWICE

THE NAUGHTY LIST

CLAIRE HASTINGS

In loving memory of Denali -
You are loved and missed more than you will ever know. See you
on the other side of the rainbow bridge, Bubba.

PROLOGUE

ONE WOULD HAVE to be living under a rock to not have seen the now-viral interview featuring beloved Adored Network actress Hollie Berry and Lyle Tucker on *Wake Up LA*.

The country is divided on Berry's reactions to Tucker's questions and her abrupt firing from Adored Network. The girl next door known for her sweet and romantic Christmas movies shocked millions when she loudly proclaimed that she was "claiming her coal" instead of apologizing for her off-brand behavior at a Vegas nightclub.

What does that phrase mean? Why has it become the top trending hashtag on every social media platform? Why has #ClaimYourCoal become the new battle cry of women around the world?

US Daily has received the full video of the interview between Berry and Tucker and has transcribed it below. This includes the un-aired portion where Berry stormed off the set.

Is Berry justified in her actions? Are Adored Network and Tucker? You can decide for yourself.

LYLE TUCKER: Thank you for being on the show. I must

say, not everyone can be as beautiful as you, especially after the weekend you had.

HOLLIE BERRY: Thanks for having me! It's great to be here.

LT: The last forty-eight hours for you I'm sure have been a whirlwind. Do you have anything to say regarding your behavior this weekend? Some are saying that your actions may have put you on Santa's naughty list…

HB: (Laughing) The naughty list… It was my best friend's bachelorette party, but the images and videos were taken completely out of context.

LT: Then please, what was the original context? Because from what the world has seen in a video that now has more than three million views, it looks like you were having sex on stage with a male stripper.

HB: Well, that's a little dramatic considering I was fully clothed and he was still in his Tarzan loincloth. There was absolutely no sex involved with our weekend.

LT: Thank you for bringing that up. The selfie of you next to a half-naked man is a little off-brand for you, don't you think? You're the sweetheart of the Adored Network, known for their sweet and romantic movies. What has Adored said to you about your behavior in terms of the video and photo?

HB: The dancer is a fan of my movies. He and his husband watch them every year on the network. He asked for a selfie afterward. I have *never* told a fan no if they want a picture. And as far as the network goes, Adored hasn't said a thing. My private life is mine to do what I want with, as long as it doesn't go against my contract. And attending a dance performance certainly isn't forbidden.

LT: A dance performance? You call men dancing for women in nothing but their underwear a dance performance? Sounds more like a strip club to me.

HB: It wasn't a strip club. Naked Heat is a dance performance. It's not like we were there to throw dollar bills around.

LT: Even so, you had to know that the Adored Network would not be happy with how you are spending your free time.

HB: Well, I think that's kind of the point. It's MY free time. And I wanted to spend MY free time celebrating my best friend's bachelorette party.

LT: Actually, we have a bit of breaking news here. I've just been handed a press release from the Adored Network saying that they are terminating your contract with the network for breaking a morality clause and are canceling your next three movies. What is your reaction to this?

HB: … Um, obviously I don't know anything about that.

LT: Well, it's true. Viewers at home, you are now seeing a photo of the press release that was just sent out by Adored.

HB: (long pause) I'm sorry, this is the press release? Like they just sent this out without even notifying me first? If that's true, then I guess you'll need to speak to my lawyer. I don't think I should comment on this without—

LT: But Hollie, you have to have some feelings about this? These movies you make for Adored made your career and, frankly, are the only reason people even know who you are. You have to have something to say about this decision?

HB: Yeah, I have some feelings. Pretty specific feelings. If that's an actual press release, I think it's pretty (expletive removed) that they would do that without contacting me first.

LT: Please, Hollie, watch your tone and words. And of course it's an actual press release. Do you think we would lie to you? We aren't the ones being questioned about our moral standards.

HB: MY moral standards? I've lived in Hollywood for 20 years with a squeaky-clean image. Do you have any idea how hard that is? I don't party; I don't sleep around. I do my job, and I'm good at it. God forbid I go to a bachelorette party! How about your moral standards? You like publicly shaming women for something every man in America has done. How does that line up with your moral compass?

LT: My moral compass isn't being questioned here. I wasn't the one who, as it has been described by numerous media outlets and tabloids, dry humped a man in front of hundreds of other women. What kind of message does that say to other women or young girls who consider you a role model? Is that the kind of moral standard you want to set for them?

HB: Yeah, you know what? It is! If women want to take control of their sexuality, I say go for it! Why do men like you get to decide what's okay? I didn't dry hump anyone in Vegas, but if I had, that would be my choice. You want to know about *my* message to women and girls? Here it is. Go out there and make the world your (expletive deleted). If this puts me on the naughty list then so be it. I'll take all the coal. Hell, I'll proudly claim my coal!

LT: You just lost your biggest contract. You are a viral video. Do you really think encouraging women and girls to, as you said, claim their coal, is the best thing you can do right now?

HB: No. The best thing I can do is this... (muffled noises) I'll show you what claiming my coal looks like, you ignorant... (muffled noises)

At this point in the interview, Hollie Berry removed her microphone. So while we can't know exactly what she said to Mr. Tucker as a parting shot, the middle finger salute she gave him as she stormed off stage was pretty clear.

CHAPTER ONE

THERE WAS magic in the air.

Haven Taylor could feel it. Swirling around her like pixie dust in a cartoon, a whisper against her skin, making her feel all tingly inside. This time of year did that to her. There was just something about it. She didn't care what anyone said, Christmas magic was real.

Humming "All I Want For Christmas Is You," she turned the corner into the teachers' lounge. She had forty-five minutes until her first graders were done with the last art class before the holiday break, and she couldn't wait to see the masterpieces they brought back with them. Each one was sure to be a mishmash of ill-formed shapes, cotton balls that weren't properly glued to the construction paper, and covered in more glitter than was ever necessary—the pieces were crafted by six-year-olds after all. But the extreme joy that radiated off each one of them as they showed off their work, telling her all about how they couldn't wait to get home and give it to a certain family member, made it all worth it. Even the glitter.

The sound of laughter wafted through the air, greeting

her, making the happiness she was feeling bubble up even more. They were two days from the winter break, and everyone—students and teachers alike—was on the edge of their seat waiting for that last bell. As much as Haven loved her students, she was looking forward to the two weeks off and time at home with her family.

"There's Miss Taylor!" Doug Schwartz, one of the other first-grade teachers, called with his arms raised high in the air, like he was signaling a field goal kick was good. "We were starting to wonder if you got lost on your way back from the art room."

"Nope, just stopped to potty. I couldn't hold it any longer," she said with a laugh, taking a seat in the open spot at the table.

The scheduling gods had smiled down on the first grade this year, with all five classes' special period lining up during the same slot, leaving all five teachers free at the exact same time. In theory they should have used this time to catch up on grading or other admin work, but they never did. Whenever asked about it, Emily Conrad, who had the room right next to Haven, would always reason it away with the answer of "we're having a grade-level meeting."

"Potty. You're so cute," Lynn Ames giggled.

"What did I miss?" Haven asked. "What was so funny?"

"Hollie Berry," Mike Hill answered, holding up a copy of *US Daily*.

America's Sweetheart was front and center on the cover of the rag-mag, her long blonde waves flowing over her bare shoulders, showing off her perfectly toned arms in a white tank top with gold trim on the collar. It was a semirecent photo of the star, and had been featured on the cover of a couple of magazines in the last few months. Her sky-blue eyes sparkled, giving off the vibe that she was totally your BFF. In Haven's mind, she was the epitome of a modern woman. She had grace, class, and was her own woman. Everything that Haven wanted to be.

"I love her. I mean, seriously. Not at all ashamed to admit my girl crush on her," Haven declared, taking the magazine from Mike.

Flipping through the pages, she quickly located the article in question. There was no doubt it had something to do with the pictures that surfaced of Hollie recently at a bachelorette party in Vegas, where she had taken a photo with one of the performers. The whole thing was being blown out of proportion online, with people claiming that Hollie was up there having sex with them. Haven had seen videos of a Naked Heat performance online. Was it sexy? Sure was. But it also wasn't anything more than what would be shown in a movie.

Skimming over the article to make sure it wasn't anything she hadn't already read, Haven giggled out loud reading Hollie's statement about how "there was absolutely no sex involved with our weekend."

You and me both, Hollie...there is no sex involved in my weekends right now either...

"Really?" Doug questioned.

"Ummm, have you met me? I love all things Adored Network, but especially Hollie. I've seen all her movies like a million times. And I do mean *all* of them. Like, back to the *Head to Mistletoe* days. *Chasing Snowflakes* is my ultimate though. I watch it every year on Christmas Eve. And maybe a couple of other times too. Oh! And that red-and-green-tartan skater dress I was wearing the other day? It's almost exactly like the one that Hollie wore in *All Snowed Inn*, when she got up on stage and serenaded Ian Brock. Only difference is that mine had that cinch around the waist and hers didn't."

Haven took a breath, the words rushing out of her faster than she had intended.

"That part I got. But after all this…" Doug gestured at the magazine. "I would have thought someone like you would have, like, disowned her."

Disowned her?

Haven's brow crinkled, her face showing off all the confusion that was going through her head. Why on earth would she disown Hollie over this?

"You lost me."

"The whole Vegas thing. She's not the nice girl anymore. Landed herself squarely on the naughty list."

"She can land squarely on my lap," Mike muttered, waggling his eyebrows. He was known for being the crass one of the group—at least behind the scenes. When he was with the kids, it was like watching the guy on *Blue's Clues*. He reminded her of her brother in that way, and her excitement to go home for the holidays and see him resurfaced.

"Don't be an ass, Mike," Lynn chirped, smacking him with the back of her hand. He shrugged, a look on his face letting them know he refused to feel guilty over his comment, earning him a laugh.

"She went to her best friend's bachelorette party."

"She was seen having *s-e-x* on stage," Doug stage whispered, pretending to be scandalized. Leaning forward, he continued, "with the strippers."

"Now you sound like my grandmother," Emily laughed.

"Dancers. Naked Heat is a male dance review," Haven corrected. "You really mean to tell me you've never seen Chippendales? And I know you guys have been to strip clubs."

"We have, sure," Mike said with a shrug. "But you?" he scoffed.

Haven gave him an indignant look. Sure, she hadn't actually been to a strip club. Or seen the Chippendales, or Naked Heat. At least not in person. But she had online—that counted, right?

"What's that supposed to mean?"

"It's just that, you're...so..." Emily trailed off.

"Pure," Mike said.

Pure...

"Pure...pure..." Haven repeated, not sure what else to say.

The word made steam erupt from Haven's ears. As if someone had put her on an open flame, everything inside her heated up, spilling over. Her tongue felt thick as she tried to form a response, unable to spew out everything that was suddenly boiling inside her. Who said that to someone? Mike, apparently. Which only made it worse, since they all knew that he was a bit of a playboy. Haven had never considered herself a feminist, but to sit here and be given a so-called compliment straight out of the 1800s was making her reconsider her stance.

"That doesn't sound creepy at all," Lynn commented, looking up from her phone.

Mike shrugged, leaning back in his chair with his arms crossed and resting against his chest. Lynn rolled her eyes, turning back to her phone. Haven looked from one coworker to the next, waiting for someone to say something. Anything. They couldn't really just leave it like that, could they?

"It's that...and I say this with love," Doug said. "You're a Goody Two-Shoes."

"Goody Two-Shoes?!" Haven exclaimed, louder than she had intended.

A Goody Two-Shoes. That was almost worse than being called pure. Almost.

"Doug's right," Lynn added. "You're Little Miss Perfect. Everything is always neat and tidy, you have all the cute little sayings and posters in your classroom, and your reports are always done on time. You just used the word potty for crying out loud! To a bunch of grown-ups. I mean, c'mon."

"I'm in school mode. School mode Haven uses words like potty. Because she talks to six-year-olds all day."

"Yeah, but…" Lynn sighed. "You're just…if this were *Grease*, you'd be Sandy."

"Can I be Rizzo?" Doug chirped.

"No," Lynn and Emily answered in unison.

"Have you ever stepped out of line? Even once?" Lynn asked. Her voice was calm and friendly, despite her borderline accusatory words.

"Of course I have!" Haven defended. She wanted to give them an example. Problem was, nothing was coming to mind.

She had broken the rules. She wasn't always the good girl. Her coworkers had no idea what she did on her own time. No idea what her life was like. Sure, it wasn't all that interesting, since she didn't have many friends in Atlanta, having only moved here over the summer. Back home, she'd had a life. It didn't involve male dancers and trips to Vegas, but how were they to know that? It could have.

And as for her classroom, of course it had fun sayings and posters. She was a first-grade teacher. That is what first-grade teachers did! Puppies, kittens, and baby bunnies were almost essential in her line of work. As was using the word "potty."

"You have no idea what I do when I'm not here," she continued, still feeling all kinds of defensive. "I could be a wild child just pretending to be the nice girl."

"This is usually where I would make a comment about how it's always the quiet ones," Mike chirped. "But you're wearing a dress with smiling, dancing snow people on it. There isn't a wild child in there."

Haven glanced down at her dress, letting her eyes settle

on a pair of snow people who were indeed in the middle of some kind of dance. In her mind it had always been the foxtrot, but she supposed it could have been anything. Which was only proving everyone's point.

She was wearing a dress with dancing cartoons. There was nothing badass about it. She was absolutely the good girl. But no more. If Hollie Berry could go out and celebrate in her own way, Haven Taylor could too.

She just had to figure out how.

Pushing up from the table quickly, Haven knocked over the chair she'd been sitting in, the loud crash of it hitting the floor reverberating through the room. Stepping around it, she started for the door. Part of her felt guilty for just leaving it there, but this was her first step in shaking off her goody-goody ways. Or at least trying to.

"Where are you going?" Emily asked.

"I'm going to take a lesson from the Hollie Berry play-book, and land myself on the naughty list!"

"Land yourself on the naughty list? What's that even supposed to mean?" Doug questioned.

Haven spun around, hands landing on her hips, a coy smile tugging at her lips. Staring down each one of her coworkers, she sucked in a breath, finding confidence she hadn't known was there.

"I'm off to claim my coal."

CHAPTER TWO

"Isn't that Haven?"

D.B. Elliot let out a groan that could almost be heard over the crowd at Bunz, a local hot spot and the unofficial hangout for the Atlanta Rising Football Club. The sports bar might have been designed to target women, but since the team's owner was friends with the owner of the bar, the players had adopted it as their own as well. Which is how Elliot ended up in a corner booth as his teammate harassed him.

"It is, isn't it?" Chance Walker asked again, nodding toward the bar.

"For the last time, I don't have a thing for my best friend's little sister."

That was a lie. Because he most certainly did have a *thing* for Haven Taylor. A very big thing. But that was going to remain a very big secret.

"You can keep denying it all you want, but that isn't what I asked."

"Did you see Haven is at the bar?" Liam Daley, their

goalie, slipped into the booth, his Irish accent so thick his words sounded jumbled together thanks to all the noise.

For fuck's sake...

"Which one is she?" Link, their shirtless waiter who had been leaning against their table, asked as he twisted to see.

"The cute little brunette in the red dress at the corner of the bar," Chance answered, nodding that way.

Elliot's head whipped in that direction, confirming it was indeed the sweet-natured girl who had been filling his dreams longer than he cared to admit. Her head was resting in her hand, her attention focused on the notebook in front of her. No doubt one of the ones she always kept in that large tote bag of hers, with some cute cartoon animal on it. She was wearing what he knew to be one of her favorite winter dresses, one that always made her giggle whenever she talked about it. Although missing from this scene was that radiant smile that matched said giggle. In fact, she almost looked...sad.

"She is cute," Link commented.

She's more than cute...she's...perfect.

"I should go say hi," Elliot muttered, trying to sound nonchalant. He knew he didn't though, and that his buddies were never going to let him live it down.

"Yeah, go say hi," Chance replied. The look on his face said it all. He knew exactly what Elliot was up to. Fuck.

"While you're over there, tell Dash that if he doesn't stop flirting with his girlfriend, I'm ordering for him and he's stuck with whatever I pick. I already know Mahoney's order, so that's not an excuse to delay this. He can see Talia after we eat. I'm starving," Liam added.

Elliot nodded, only half listening. He had no intention of grabbing their hotshot striker. He had a mission. He needed to know why Haven looked like someone kicked her puppy.

Making his way across the bar, he set his sights on his

favorite elementary school teacher. He couldn't name whatever it was that was so captivating about Haven. Everything about her made him want more. More of her laugh, more of her energy, more of *her*. She'd had him wrapped around her finger since they were kids.

"This one looks like he's copping a feel...right here," Elliot said in a low voice from behind Haven, poking her in the side as he said it.

Haven let out a squeal, jumping in her seat. Spinning around, eyes as big as the moon, her surprised face morphed into a smile when she realized it was him. There was still something missing in that smile though, making Elliot's stomach sink.

"Dobby!"

Dobby...

Elliot's heart squeezed as Haven threw her arms around his neck, her personal nickname for him still ringing in his ears. No one ever called him by his full name—always opting for the initials—ever since he had started insisting on it in the second grade. Well, everyone but Haven, who had been calling him Dobby since she could talk.

Haven let go, cool air slipping in between them, making Elliot miss the feel of her body against his almost instantly. He wished more than anything he had an excuse to continue to hold on to her, but anything he could come up with just seemed creepy. She looked at him like another big brother. Always had, always would.

"Whatcha working on?" he asked, peering over her shoulder and trying to catch a glimpse of her notebook as she slid back onto her stool. "Let me guess. You're going to be making sugar plum fairies during the first-grade Christmas party tomorrow, and you're putting the finishing touches on your design."

"No, nothing like that," she answered, forcing a brief

smile. Elliot could tell it wasn't entirely sincere though, the wistful look in her eye giving her away. "Just something personal."

"Personal?"

What on earth could be so personal that she wouldn't talk about it? This was Haven; she was an open book. She'd never been one to hold anything back. Like when they were teenagers and she'd rattle on about her period, sharing way more than he or her brother, Hudson, had ever wanted to know. That was only one example—over the years she had come to him with all sorts of things, from boys, to school, to how to properly stretch a muscle. If she could tell him about her period or ask him about losing her virginity, what on earth could be so private now?

Haven nodded. He was now officially intrigued. Opening his mouth to ask, Haven blurted out a question, talking over him.

"Am I too pure to be pink?"

What?! "Is that question supposed to make sense?"

"You know, like in *Grease*. How they make fun of Sandy because she's a Goody Two-Shoes. Is that me? Am I a Goody Two-Shoes?"

The tears forming in her eyes as she asked the question tugged at Elliot's heart. He hated seeing her so upset. He had no idea who'd told her this, but right now he wanted to beat them senseless. Haven was a lot of things. She was sunshine and rainbows—an infectious bundle of energy that brightened every room she walked into. She even had a way of cheering up his grumpy ass. She loved kids and teaching, and he was pretty sure she'd never met a stranger. In other words, she was perfect.

"Who the hell told you that?"

"Everyone."

"Everyone?"

"Well, all the other teachers in my grade. They said I was a goody-goody. They made fun of the way I dress—"

"Because you sometimes look like Miss Frizzle?"

Haven scowled at him. "I would kill for her solar system dress, you know that."

"I do. But what does this have to do with…" he trailed off, glancing over at the notebook once again. "A naughty list?"

"Yes, I'm making my own naughty list. It's not like I need to be a bad girl, or suddenly channel my inner Jayne Mansfield. I just don't want to be a Goody Two-Shoes. Hollie Berry is right; it's time to claim my coal."

"So you made a list of all the naughty things you want to do?"

"Pretty much."

Elliot picked up the notebook, his eyes scanning down the list.

Buy a sex toy

Streaking

Watch porn - R

Take a naughty photo (Lingerie? Nude?)

Fool around in public - R

Visit a strip club

Sex tape - R

Strip poker - R

Whip cream bikini - R

Go commando

Kiss under the mistletoe – R

One-Night Stand

One-night stand…Haven wants to have a one-night stand…

Elliot blinked, hard, trying to regain his focus. He couldn't zero in on that. Couldn't let his mind run wild with what it would be like to get tangled up in the sheets, her beautiful chestnut hair cascading over the pillow, her choco-late-brown eyes halfway hidden behind her lids as they fluttered from the pleasure rippling through her…

"Ahem," he coughed. So much for playing this cool. "Why is there an R next to some of these items?"

"Oh, those are relationship ones."

"Relationship ones?"

"Yes, a naughty list for when I'm in a relationship. Like 'watch porn.' I can look up whatever I want on the Internet by myself, but the idea there is to watch it *with* someone. And that just feels more relationship-y."

Right…

"So then, the nonrelationship-y ones…you're going to do those? When?"

"This weekend. Our flight home isn't until Monday, so I have time. Tomorrow is a half day for students, and Friday is a teacher workday. The only other thing on my calendar is the Atlanta Rising Christmas party Saturday night, so that's like three and a half days."

"Three and a half days to…buy a sex toy, go streaking, take a naughty photo, visit a strip club, go commando and have a one-night stand?"

"Maybe not all those things, but most of them. The one-night stand will be the hardest, but that's why I'm at Bunz. I thought…OMG!" Her eyes went wide, her mouth hanging open in an O shape, those soulful brown eyes lighting up. Elliot knew this look. This was the look she got whenever she had a bright idea. The same one she'd had when she'd come up with the idea that landed him in the eighth-grade talent show. She was up to something. "You!"

"Me?"

"Yes, you! Dobby, it's perfect! You can be the person to help me do all these things."

Her sweet giggle rang out. Despite the noise in the bar,

Elliot heard it loud and clear, his dick reacting to the sound. Fuck, if it wasn't bad enough that he'd just been picturing her naked in his bed, now she was giggling. She continued that and he would be putty in her hands.

"I don't see why you can't just do these yourself."

"Because I need someone else for the one-night stand, duh!"

"You want us to have a one-night stand?"

Nope, no way. That's where he drew the line. He couldn't sleep with her. Despite the fact that said fantasy was a regular contributor to his spank bank, he couldn't make it a reality. She was his best friend's little sister. "Haven, I adore you, but you're out of your mind. We can't sleep together. It's a bad idea on so many levels. Not the least of which is that Hudson would have me drawn and quartered."

"He doesn't have to know. It could be our secret. Besides, I'm pretty sure that if he had to pick someone for me to have a one-night stand with, it would be the guy who has been his best friend since kindergarten."

Elliot sighed. "Haven…"

"You don't want to," she muttered. Nodding solemnly, she shrank into herself, her whole body looking crestfallen. It was the same look he'd noticed on her earlier from across the bar—but worse. Because this time, he was the one who had kicked her puppy. "I'll find someone else, don't worry. Like him."

She jutted her chin out in the direction from which he'd come just a moment ago. Twisting around to see who she was looking at, Elliot felt his blood pressure rise. Walking toward them, confident smirk on his pretty face, was Link. The former professional dancer looked like he'd walked right off a billboard, ready to seduce the pants off any woman who looked at him. He probably could too. As a dancer, it was clear he had moves Elliot couldn't begin to fathom. Moves that he would put on Haven.

No, just no.

Link was a nice enough guy. Elliot enjoyed hanging out with him, but that didn't mean he was good enough for Haven. No one was good enough for her.

Elliot couldn't let Haven sleep with him. Or anyone else.

Haven deserved to be treated like a queen, even if it was a one-and-done thing. No one on this earth was going to treat her like he would.

"Fine. I'll do it."

"Really?"

"Really." Pulling his phone from his pocket, he snapped a photo of her list. He had some planning to do. "I'll text you tomorrow with some details on getting this whole thing started."

"OMG, Dobby, thank you so much!" Launching herself off the stool again, her arms were around his neck in an instant, her soft lips pressing a chaste kiss on his cheek. "You won't regret this, I promise!"

God...I hope not...

CHAPTER THREE

THE TEXT that Haven found waiting on her phone after all her kiddos had been picked up and sent home was simple and straightforward. But that didn't make it any less confusing.

Dobby: Club entrance at Pemberton 7p. Be there ;)

Haven knew the set of doors he was talking about. Pemberton was the brand-new, state-of-the-art stadium where the Atlanta Rising played all their home matches, and it had a special side entrance for the club level. Elliot had gotten her a special pass to attend his games and cheer for him, giving her a spot in the section where all the players' families sat and access through this dedicated entrance. Why she needed to meet him here now was beyond her though. The season was over.

The cold winter wind whipped around her as she approached the building, sending a chill through her. Worry crept up her spine as she looked around, not seeing Elliot. It

20

was cold and dark out, and she didn't love the idea of standing outside waiting for him. Especially since she had no idea what he had up his sleeve.

She had to admit though, she was excited. No, excited wasn't the right word. Giddy—that was it. She'd barely slept last night thinking about how much fun this was going to be. Thankfully today had been a short day at school, filled with the grade-level holiday parties, since she was sure that she wouldn't have been able to concentrate on actually teaching. Thoughts of sex toys and streaking were the last thing that needed to make an appearance in front of her students.

Suddenly, one of the doors to the stadium opened and Elliot appeared, his finger held vertically to his mouth, signaling her to be quiet. Ushering her inside, he smiled a devilish smile, making the chill from the wind start to disappear.

"Hi," she whispered. "What are we doing here? Isn't the stadium closed? How did you get in?"

"Don't ask questions you don't want the answer to."

Elliot winked. A giggle bubbled up inside, escaping before Haven could stop herself, and her hands flew to her mouth, like she could somehow manage to put the sound back in there. There was just too much joy and excitement simmering inside her. Elliot shook his head, silently laughing, gesturing for her to follow him. She did as instructed, her eyes adjusting to the dark as they weaved their way through a corridor she'd never seen. This wasn't the way to the seats she normally sat in, but an underground maze leading them to the unknown. Or at least unknown to her. Elliot knew exactly where they were, and she trusted him.

"Ready?" he asked, still whispering.

Haven nodded quickly, her heart pounding so fast she was sure it was going to give them away. Elliot winked again, taking her hand, tugging her around a corner toward a light. A few more steps, and Haven recognized where she was.

The pitch.

It was still mostly dark, the only light coming from the few dim emergency bulbs around the stands, but it was enough for her to be able to see the field. The massive green turf was overwhelming from this angle, sending her mind reeling.

"What are we doing here?"

"Item number one on your naughty list—streaking," he told her, that devilish smile in full force. The dim light caught his sandy-colored hair just enough to make it shimmer. "I figured it was a little too cold to do it outside, being the end of December and all, so I thought indoors would be best. Streaking across the pitch is something some people can only dream of, and here's your chance. Only you won't go to jail or be majorly fined for it."

"Unless we get caught for breaking and entering?"

"Well, yeah. But now you can add that to your naughty list as well."

Haven bit back another giggle—something she was sure she'd be doing for the rest of the night. They were really doing this.

"So, what first?"

"You…you strip," he choked out. His voice was tense, but Haven couldn't tell if that was from the awkwardness of her stupid question or something else.

"*We* strip."

"We?"

"Yes, you're doing this with me. That was the deal."

"Right. So, we strip."

Nodding, she turned around, shrugging out of her coat.

Really, you turned around? You're about to run across the field with him naked, but he can't see you unhook your bra?

Making quick work of undressing, Haven sucked in a breath. Why the hell was she so nervous? There was no one she trusted more on this earth than Elliot. He and Hudson were five years old—making her two—when Elliot's family moved in just before the boys started kindergarten and decided they were inseparable. He had never *not* been a part of her life. Which is what made him the perfect partner in this little adventure.

"Daubney Blake Winston Elliot!" she hissed. "Why are you still wearing underwear?"

Elliot looked down at his body, then back up at her, confusion on his face. "Did you just full name me? I can't remember the last time someone full named me."

"I did just full name you, because you are still in your skivvies!"

Haven stomped her foot, like a horse expressing its displeasure, hands resting on her bare hips. Elliot's eyes flew to her breasts, her nipples tightening under his gaze. A twinge of self-consciousness flowed through her as his eyes danced up and down her naked form. Did he like what he saw? When his eyes met hers again, he lightly licked his lips, sending a whole new rush through her.

Stop it; this is Dobby...

"Only because you undressed faster than I did," he answered.

His eyes remained glued on hers as he hooked his thumbs under the waistband of his boxer briefs, shimmying them down. Haven swallowed hard, trying not to break their stare, but she couldn't help it. The second the dark fabric hit the turf, her eyes flew to his crotch, taking in D.B. Elliot in all his glory. And it was a hell of a sight.

Long and thick, it was hands down the biggest penis she'd ever seen. It was like something out of a magazine, the picture of perfection.

She needed a change of topic…bad.

"Speaking of your full name, I get why you dropped Daubney. It's weird. Yes, I know it's your grandmother's maiden name, but still, it's weird to be a first name. But I've never understood why you don't just go by Blake," she said, the words rushing out.

Way to make this awkward…

"Because Blake is a douchey name."

"No it's not."

"Yes, it is. Have you ever met a Blake who isn't a douchebag?" Tilting his head, he gave her a questioning look, as if to say he already knew the answer.

"My hairdresser is Blake and he's a pretty chill guy."

"Okay, so one. Hairdresser Blake is not a douche. The rest? All douchebags," he said, stepping in closer to her. Haven's heart jumped, a new feeling inside her that she couldn't name taking over. "But we didn't come here to talk about your hairdresser, or my full name."

"Nope," she replied, popping the p. Her nerves were all over the place, leaving her unsure of what to do. There was one thing she was sure of, and that was how her students would react. Time to follow their lead. Tapping him in the middle of his chest, she gave him a little push. "Tag, you're it!"

Turning on her heel, she took off running, knowing it was just a matter of time before he caught up with her. He was a professional soccer player—he ran for a living. At six one, he had plenty of height on her five-foot-six self, and there were plenty of days it seemed like his legs were as tall as she was. She, on the other hand, was quite possibly the least athletic person on earth, preferring arts and crafts to any version of exercise.

Elliot let out a groan, the sound of his feet hitting the turf and closing in on her music to her ears. She zagged, changing the direction of her path, hoping that might give her a little more time. The air inside the stadium was cool, but comfortably so, even as she moved. It made her feel alive, goose bumps trailing up her arms. She could understand why people did this, maybe not in the middle of a game with thousands of people in the stands, but there was something freeing about being like this. Or maybe it was just the thrill of knowing she wasn't supposed to be here, naked on the field.

"You can't escape!" Elliot shouted.

Throwing a look over her shoulder, she caught a glimpse of him, much closer than she had realized. She let out a squeal, trying to pick up the pace, but her little legs couldn't move any faster. A second later Elliot's arms were around her waist, pulling her flush against him as he yanked her off the ground, spinning her around.

"Not fair!"

"Is too," he said, tightening his grip. She squealed again, loving the feel of his arms around her, his warm skin soothing her. "You ran away; I had to capture you."

"I said tag, not capture the flag," she said with a laugh. "Or girl."

Placing her back down on the ground, Elliot spun her in his arms, her front pressing against his. She could feel his hardness between them, wondering if it would feel as good in her hand as it did pressed against her tummy.

Stop it...

"Thank you," she whispered.

There was so much more she wanted to say, so much more that was running through her head, but that was the only thing that seemed appropriate in the moment. She'd seen him naked before, having walked in on the boys skinny-dipping in their pool one summer during college. But there was something very different about this moment. A pull that she hadn't felt before.

"For?"

"This," she answered with a small shrug, staring up at him. His firm biceps fit perfectly in her hands as she held on to him, not daring to let go. "Helping me. For not laughing at my list."

"I won't lie; I don't understand it. But if it makes you happy, then…" he paused, one side of his mouth quirking upward. Haven felt a tingle inside her at the movement. Elliot had never been much of a smiler—always the serious one. Which made his smiles that much more potent, since they were so rare. "As long as you're happy, Haven, I'm happy."

"Tonight you have made me very happy, Dobby."

A slight, almost imperceptible movement against her skin caught Haven off guard. Was that…did his dick just twitch? No, she was imagining things. She was not having any kind of effect on his junk, no matter how badly she wanted to think she did in this moment. Except, she was pretty sure she just felt it again.

"Haven," he whispered, tightening his grip again.

Their bodies were already as close as they could be, but it still seemed too far away. Could he hear how fast her heart was beating? Did he know that she couldn't stop looking at his lips, wishing that he would kiss her? The way his head was tilted to the side, moving in closer, millimeter by millimeter, said yes, but she didn't dare believe it. It was all in her head. Right?

Pushing up on her toes, she closed that gap, expecting him to pull away. To let go of her and say something that was so big-brother-like that it would erase all these desires. Elliot did no such thing. Instead, he licked his lips, eyes turning dark. Fuck, did she want to kiss him.

Forget want. Claiming her coal was not about want. It was about doing.

She was going to kiss her brother's best friend.

"Hey!" A disembodied voice sounded, startling both of them. Jumping backward, Haven spun around trying to figure out where it came from. She soon found her answer, as a flashlight cut through the darkness. "Who's there?"

"Shit," Elliot cursed.

"Time to get dressed?"

"Yes!"

Grabbing her hand, Elliot took off, sprinting as fast as he could toward their pile of clothes. Haven did her best to keep up, but she tripped, almost taking him down with her. Elliot didn't miss a beat though, scooping her up and throwing her over his shoulder. Her laughter reverberated through the empty pitch and off the stands. Haven was unable to control herself. All she could picture was how funny they must look, naked as the day they were born, her pasty backside on full display on his shoulder.

Five minutes later, they were dressed and back outside the stadium, without having run into whichever security guard had interrupted their moment. A moment that Haven was never going to forget.

"Item number one, streaking, check!" Elliot said, miming a check mark with his finger.

"What's next?"

"You shall receive your next set of instructions tomorrow. But for now, how about hot cocoa and *All Snowed Inn*? I assume you own it?"

"That's the dumbest question anyone has ever asked me. Of course I own it."

"Then lead the way, Haven Mae Taylor." Stopping in her tracks, Haven glared at him. "You full named me earlier, so it's only fair."

He had her there. Slipping her arm into his, she continued on, sighing contently. She had more fun tonight than she could remember having in a long time. She was going to enjoy this project. Maybe too much.

She just couldn't let her heart get caught up in it.

CHAPTER FOUR

UNEASE FLOWED through Elliot like a raft down the Mississippi. This wasn't his scene to begin with. He'd been to a strip club once in his life, the day Hudson turned eighteen, which was just two weeks after he had, the two of them going just because they could. No, make that twice—his college team had stumbled into one after winning the national championship. Wait, three—a bachelor party three years ago.

Still, this was something you did with the guys. Not the girl you had a secret crush on. Certainly not your best friend's little sister.

Especially if those last two were the same person.

"O...M G..." Haven muttered, twisting in her seat, soaking in the bright lights, smoke, and whatever the fuck that smell was.

Daddy issues and vomit, most likely...

Elliot knew exactly how Haven felt; it was a lot to take in. The club was set up just like every other one he'd been in—a stage with a long runway, leading to a circular area, complete with stereotypical pole at the end, and a bar off to the side.

Folding chairs were lined up along the stage, and bigger, more comfortable leather armchairs were placed behind them. It looked just like you expected, and still somehow managed to be a surprise.

"So, how does this work? Just like the movies?" she asked, turning toward him. Her eyes were bright with wonder, her pretty pink lips holding back a smile. As much as he didn't want to be here, seeing her this excited made it worth the awkwardness.

"Pretty much. They play a song, someone will come out, strut her stuff, and that's about it."

"So, when do we toss the money? Just whenever she does something we like?"

"Yup. Although don't worry about that part."

"Are you kidding? I came prepared to participate!"

Errr...what?!

Elliot choked on the breath he was inhaling, sure he didn't hear her properly. She came prepared to participate? Before he could ask her for a correction though, she pulled out a wad of cash from her little crossbody purse, which from the looks of it was all single dollar bills.

Letting out a sigh of relief that she had meant tipping and not actually performing, he turned his attention back toward the dancer who was busy twerking for a set of suits off to their left. His pulse was rushing, mind still locked on the idea of what Haven would look like up there, under these lights, in nothing but her heels and a thong. Knowing her, the thong would be covered in something girlie and cute like pink polka dots—the thought of which was making his dick harder than it should. Fuck, now he was never going to be able to see pink polka dots without thinking of this.

"This is wild," Haven said, looking around. "And I know wild...I teach the first grade."

"Sometimes I wonder if you listen to yourself talk. Isn't

the whole point of this list...the whole reason we're even here tonight...because you *aren't* wild?"

"Not wild as in crazy," she corrected. "Wild as in intense. And in that way, the first grade is *wild*."

Elliot just stared at her. Fuck, she was cute. Forget whatever woman was up on stage twerking, the sweet brunette next to him was all he cared about.

"Yes, the first grade is widely known for its sheer intensity."

Haven smacked him with the back of her hand, her beautiful features scrunched into a playful scowl. She was used to his grumpiness and overflowing sarcasm after more than twenty years of friendship. Somehow, it never seemed to get to her. Probably because she viewed him as another older brother.

"You don't have to believe me, but it is. For crying out loud, you're learning how to be a human! Things like how to write stuff down and how to manage friendships and deal with people you don't like. Oh, and following rules—that's a big one. Rules that sometimes just don't make sense. All while your teeth are falling out! That's a lot to ask of anyone. Much less someone who is six."

Giving him a smug look, knowing that she had made her point, she turned back to the performance, immediately mesmerized by what she was seeing. Elliot couldn't blame her—it was a sight to see. The current dancer was suspended in the air, at least six feet up on the pole, her legs spread wide, showing off the bedazzled crotch of her panties, fingers working her nipples.

"How is she staying up there?"

"I have no idea."

"So, what do I do? Just toss the money onto the stage? Oh, what do they call that? Make it rain!" She giggled. "Hope she comes closer so that I can tip her personally?"

"Your choice," Elliot answered, swallowing hard. He still couldn't believe that he was sitting here, walking Haven through how to act at a strip club. Talk about a surreal moment. Nothing about this was comfortable. Least of all the hard-on he was still sporting. Damn pink polka dots still flooded his mind. Shifting, he tried to find a position where he was at least semicomfortable, while not advertising what exactly was going on in his pants. It was a task much more difficult than he had anticipated.

Haven giggled, tossing a handful of singles onto the stage. The sound went straight to his groin. So much for getting comfortable. The smile on her face was worth it though. She seemed to be having a great time—soaking in the novelty of being the only woman in here, on top of checking the item off her list.

"You know who she looks like," Haven commented.

"Who? The girl on the pole?"

Haven nodded. "Bettany."

"Bettany?"

"That girl you dated right after college. The one with the crazy eyes. Lost her mind when you were traded from New England to Minnesota, even though she was still in North Carolina at school."

"You mean Bethany."

"Nope, Bettany. She used to snarl and correct me every time I slipped and said 'Bethany.'"

Elliot bit back a smile, keeping his gaze trained on the stage. He would have sworn the girl's name was Bethany, but he trusted Haven more than he did his own memory. Because she was right—his ex did have crazy eyes. And that fit she mentioned? That had been the final straw. Regardless, he liked that she disliked the women that had previously been in his life. Lord knows he hated the guys who had been in hers.

"Better than that guy you dated all throughout college. Paul?"

"What was wrong with Paul?"

"Where do I start? How about the fact that he kept talking about your education degree being useful when you home-school your minimum of six kids?"

"I would love a big family. Six might be a bit much, but three or four would be a good number. And he would have gotten over the whole homeschooling part," she said, dismissing his concerns. "I knew Hudson hated him; I didn't realize you did too."

Of course I hated him; he had you and I didn't...

"I certainly wasn't sad to see the back of him."

Haven let out another giggle before turning back to the stage. A new performer was up, this one showing off a floor routine Elliot was sure would not be making it into the Olympics this summer. Sitting back, he forced himself to relax. Easier said than done. They were only two items into the list, and from here the list only got more complicated.

He'd spent most of the last two days trying to work out if she'd really been serious about the one-night stand. She hadn't brought it up since she'd shown him the list, making him wonder if she was reconsidering it. Either way, he didn't want to be the one to bring it up.

A little while later, after they had seen more than their fair share of dancers, Haven excused herself to the bathroom, which sounded like a fantastic idea to him. A moment in the men's room would give him a chance to adjust himself so that he didn't appear to be smuggling Pinocchio out in his pants. The thought occurred to him that maybe more than just adjusting might be needed—and probably wouldn't take more than a few strokes of his hand thanks to just how turned on he was—but he dismissed it quickly. He was not going to be that guy who jerked off in the strip club bathroom. He could wait until he got home, where he could lie in bed and picture Haven all he wanted.

"Hi!" she greeted as he stepped out of the bathroom, startling him. She was waiting just outside the men's room door, an impish look her on face. Elliot knew that look. She was up to something.

"Hi."

"Guess what I found in the bathroom?"

"That's a loaded question given where we are."

"Dobby!"

Elliot laughed, unable to hold back at the shock on her face. "Let's head to the car and you can tell me all about your new discovery."

"You make it sound like I was Marie Curie discovering radioactivity or something."

The winter air hit hard as he held the door open for her to exit the club. He hadn't realized just how warm it had been inside, a shiver running through him. Rushing Haven to the car, he clicked the button on his fob twice, getting the car started and jogging ahead to open her door for her.

"So, what did you find in the bathroom of a strip club?"

"This!"

Haven shoved a bright-blue piece of paper at him, her excitement palpable. He took it from her, already wary of what it contained. Eyes skimming the text, he let out a sigh of relief.

"Pole-dancing lessons?"

"Yes!"

"You want to take pole-dancing lessons?"

"They host them every Sunday afternoon. We can add it to the list. One last thing before we head back to Boise on Monday morning."

"You're insane."

"I am not. It's the perfect way to end our weekend!"

Elliot let out a long exhale, forcing out all the breath he had. They were supposed to be checking items off the list, not putting more things on. But in true Haven fashion, she was beaming from ear to ear, light seeming to pour out of every surface of her body from all her enthusiasm. It was infectious. And impossible to say no to.

"What time on Sunday?"

"Noon, so we can still sleep in after the Christmas party and…"

"And…"

"Our one-night stand."

And there it was.

"That's tomorrow night?" he asked, trying to sound coy, and not like he'd been thinking about it.

Haven nodded. "After the Atlanta Rising Christmas party. I figured it would be easiest since we'll already be together and all dressed up and all that. We can go, have fun at the party, and then go home and…have more fun."

Her impish smile returned, a slight blush creeping up her cheeks, despite how matter-of-factly she'd stated her plans to bed him just for the night. His dick twitched, full of new excitement.

"Okay then. If you think that you're going to have enough energy after a night with me, then sign us up."

"Really?" she squealed.

Launching herself over the center console, Haven grabbed his face, pushing her lips against his. The move caught him by surprise, his mouth taking an extra second to respond.

Holy fuck, he was kissing Haven Taylor.

Just as quickly as her mouth had met his, she started to pull away. Whether her intention was just a quick peck or if she had realized what she had done and was trying to undo it, he wasn't sure. What he did know was that he hadn't had enough. He wanted more of her. So much more.

Slipping his hand behind her neck, he pulled her closer, deepening the kiss. She kissed him back with so much fervor he no longer wondered if she had kissed him by mistake. This was anything but a mistake. He twisted his fingers in her hair, nibbling on her bottom lip, trying to slow down her movements. He wanted to enjoy this. Wanted to make this moment last. Her lips were soft and full, tasting just as sweet as he'd always imagined. Time seemed to stand still, his whole body coming alive as she whimpered into the kiss as his tongue found hers.

Fuck, could she kiss. For a second, he wondered where she had learned this, or if it came naturally to her—the same way she drove him wild with everything else she did. But the longer he kissed her, the less it mattered. All that mattered now was that she was his. At least in this moment.

A moment that was everything he'd dreamed it would be and more. One he never wanted to end. But he knew it couldn't last. Shouldn't last. Haven deserved more than a make-out session in a random parking lot. As far as first kisses went, this was a damn good one, except for the location. He would have to do better for their next one.

Gently releasing her, he sat back, running his fingers softly across her cheek. Haven stared back at him for a moment, mouth agape, breath heavy. He could see her mind running wild, trying to figure out what to say, how to react to what had just transpired.

"I should get you home; we have a big day tomorrow," he said, filling the silence. "But more than that, you deserve a proper kiss goodnight."

CHAPTER FIVE

Tingles.

Looking up at the glittery, illuminated sign, Haven understood where the store got its name. Her whole body was tingling with…something. Excitement? Nerves? She wasn't really sure. Either way, she couldn't wait for whatever today —and tonight—had in store.

"Are you coming?" Elliot asked, nodding inside as he held the door open for her.

"That seems like a loaded question, considering we haven't even gotten started," she sassed, unable to help herself. Growing up, Hudson and Elliot had never missed the opportunity to make some kind of joke out of the question he'd just asked, so it felt like second nature now to make a crack in return. See, she could do this naughty thing.

"I walked right into that," he muttered. "And someone brought her sass today."

"Sure did."

She'd woken up feeling more than just sassy. All because of him.

Three steps into the store and Haven stopped dead in her tracks. Her eyes went wide as she took in the...stuff. She didn't have a different word for it. Every inch of the store was covered in something. From clothing to toys, posters, movies, you name it. All of it erotic in nature. Sucking her lips into her mouth, she bit back a nervous laugh. She might be a very mature adult, but that didn't make her feel any less awkward about the massive penis mural on the wall directly in front of them.

"What are we looking for?" Elliot asked, glancing around, trying to be nonchalant. Haven could see how tense he was and wished she had some way to comfort him. Under normal circumstances she would slip her hand into his, giving it a squeeze to let him know she was there. Or wrap her arms around one of his and rest her head on his shoulder. But these weren't normal circumstances. She wasn't sure anything about them would ever be normal again.

Not after that kiss.

Kisses. Just as he had promised, he'd dropped her off at her door, wrapping his arms around her, holding her close, and delivering one of the most intense kisses she'd ever experienced. No, that wasn't right. The most intense kiss. She'd felt that thing in her toes. She'd thought their kiss in the car had been perfect, at least until he kissed her again. This time, her world stopped. Everything melted away with his arms cocooning her in the most glorious embrace ever. She hadn't been able to think for a solid two minutes after he'd pulled away, opened her door, and ushered her inside. Her brain had kicked into high gear not long after he'd left though. And she hadn't thought about anything else since.

Except maybe what else he could do with that tongue.

"I don't know really." Wandering farther into the store, she ambled down an aisle, full of very realistic looking replica penises. She couldn't help but wonder who the model for these had been, and if this person knew exactly what they had lent their junk to.

"What are your others like? Are you thinking something like you already have or something totally different?"

"I have no idea," she admitted. "I've never done this. I have nothing to compare any of these things to."

"Wait, you mean…" Elliot looked at her, face contorting in confusion, then morphing into realization. "Hold on, hold on, hold on."

"The only things around here to hold on to are dicks, and that seems inappropriate."

"When you put 'buy a sex toy' on your list, you meant your first?"

Given the tone of his whisper shout, Haven wasn't sure that Elliot was nearly as discreet as he thought he was being. Although discretion probably went out the window the second they walked into this place.

"That's why it's on the list," she responded, holding back the "duh!" that was rattling around in her mind. "If I already owned one, then this whole field trip would be unnecessary."

"I thought you'd just never done it in person. Like, you'd bought whatever online, being discreet. So then…how…what do you…how do you…"

Haven knew exactly what he was getting at, but she couldn't help but let him flounder. He stood there, gesturing wildly with his hands, trying to find the right words. This was the side of D.B. Elliot she had always adored the most. No, that wasn't true; she loved his wit and dry sense of humor more than anything. But there was a demure, reserved side to him that was so incredibly endearing. Although he would probably never speak to her again if he ever heard her describe him as demure. He'd been teased for being quiet and shy as a kid, and she knew that he overcompensated for that now with his grumpy exterior. Deep down though, there was her Dobby, who was one of the most thoughtful and caring men she'd ever met.

"Flick the bean?" she offered.

"Yes."

Holding up her hands, she wiggled her fingers, making jazz hands. "These magical beauties right here."

Elliot nodded, lips pressed together in a straight line. He looked like he wanted to say something but was stopping himself. That was a feeling she understood all too well at the moment. There was so much she wanted to say and do, but she was holding back. She'd been fighting the urge to kiss him all morning. Last night had left her wanting. In theory she wasn't going to be left wanting long, since they were technically scheduled to have their one-night stand tonight. Or so they had briefly discussed. Those few sentences in the car before she kissed him had been their only discussion on the topic, which made her worry that he was going to back out. Which was the very last thing she wanted.

Not just because of the list either. She wanted him. Fuck, did she want him. Even just standing here now, her eyes scanning over his body, heat and desire rushed through her. Thoughts of his beautifully muscular body looming over hers, that insanely perfect cock of his toying with her entrance, all while his mouth held hers captive in one of those soul-stealing kisses had been exactly what had pushed her over the edge not once, not twice, but *three* different times last night after she'd slipped into bed. It was a good thing she was investing in this toy, because she was pretty sure that after one night with him, it was going to get a workout.

Sauntering down the aisle a little more, she came to a

stop in front of a large, bright purple dildo. The color had been what caught her eye, making it stand out among all the different shades of beige, black, and even teal colored items. There was something else, though, that seemed *off* about it. Although, what did she know. It wasn't as if she was some kind of dildo connoisseur.

"The Big Dipper," Elliot said from behind her. Twisting around she looked at him for a brief moment, then followed his gaze to the card sitting in front of the phallus. "Fifteen inches and thick all around, this bad boy is your new best friend—"

"Fifteen inches?" Haven squeaked. "Where the hell do you put fifteen inches?"

"Well…"

"Well what? Fifteen inches, Dobby! I mean…" She huffed out a breath, still trying to wrap her mind around the physics. "Did you not pay attention in anatomy class? It's a dead-end tunnel. There is only so far you can go!"

Elliot barked out a laugh, his hand clapping over his mouth at the booming noise. She hadn't meant for it to be that funny—or funny at all. Her mind truly wanted to know exactly what was done with such a large device. Or maybe she didn't.

"Safe to say the Big Dipper is not what you're looking for."

Haven nodded, agreeing wholeheartedly. That thing would probably split her in two. Right down the middle. Like that lumberjack on the social media app ForU who was always chopping wood. Bam! Split in half. That was the last thing she needed. She was already afraid that a night with Elliot—

Haven froze, mind rushing back to the other night on the field, Elliot standing there in all his naked glory. She'd had the thought then that it was the biggest dick she'd ever seen. But just how big was it? No part of her had thought to measure it. Hell, even if she had, there wasn't a measuring tape right there.

"OMG, Dobby. You're…you're not fifteen inches, are you?"

"What?"

Haven's pulse kicked up a notch, worry suddenly rocketing through her. How had it never occurred to her to think about this? Probably because she didn't realize fifteen-inch dicks existed. No one she'd been with prior was anywhere close to that. Hell, no one she'd been with before even made her consider it not fitting. But Elliot was bigger than them, there was no doubt. At least not about his size. Fitting—well, she now had doubts about that.

"I don't think anyone has ever questioned the size of my dick," he said, shaking his head in disbelief. Closing the gap between them, his hands found her hips, the heat from them soothing. Her whole body seemed to calm from his touch, making her want to curl up into him. The fact that he hadn't run away—or worse, laughed at her—for asking was reassuring. She'd known she'd chosen the right person to do all this with, but this confirmed it even more. He'd always been there for her, and she knew he always would be. "No, I'm not fifteen inches. No one is actually fifteen inches. If some guy ever tells you he is, run."

"Actually, there is a gentleman in Mexico who is reportedly eighteen and a half inches. Although, it's a bit contested, since it's believed he used weights to stretch it. But there is a guy in New York who says his is thirteen inches and all natural," a woman said, appearing out of thin air. Her face was kind, the crooked smile matching her asymmetrical, lavender-colored hair perfectly. "I'm Natasha, owner of

Tingles. Is there something I can help with? Other than fun penis facts."

"I…errr…ahh..ummm…" Haven faltered, stepping back from Elliot and out of his grip. She missed it instantly, cool air rushing around her. A flush started to creep up the back of her neck, embarrassment kicking in. It was one thing to talk about this with Elliot, someone she loved and trusted. But a complete stranger? That might be a bridge too far.

"This is a place of acceptance, so nothing you say will be judged," Natasha said. "While something might not be your cup of tea, it might be someone else's. We're here to help people figure out what theirs might be."

"Oh, I don't mean to be insensitive. I'm glad there is a place where people can explore their…interests," Haven word vomited, suddenly unable to control herself. "I just…I mean… is there a beginners' section? Like, the kiddie pool of sex toys?"

Natasha nodded, understanding in her eyes, looking back and forth between her and Elliot a couple of times. Butterflies flitted through her tummy, liking the thought that this lady assumed they were together. Natasha knelt down, grabbing a tube-shaped package, popping right back to her feet.

"You could always just immortalize your boyfriend's," she said, handing Haven the tube that read Clone-A-Willy.

"Errr, what?" Elliot asked.

"It's a DIY kit! This could be fun!" She didn't bother to correct Natasha about the boyfriend thing. Neither did Elliot though, which made her insides sing. "You are rather…*gifted*. We could do some arts and crafts this afternoon—"

"We're not doing arts and crafts with my dick." His face was serious, but there was a glimmer in his eye that made her think that if she begged, he'd give in. Depending on how tonight went, a souvenir might not be the worst idea ever. "What else do you have for us?"

Natasha gave them a knowing wink, disappearing down the aisle for a moment, returning just as quickly, hands full of what appeared to be panties.

"These are some of our more popular items. These panties are specifically designed to hold this little vibe," she explained, holding up the two items, showing off the sewn-in pocket in the crotch where the vibrator sat. "Very discreet, look like any other pair you'd buy at a lingerie shop. The vibe is controlled by an app on your phone, and thanks to the magic of Wi-Fi, can be controlled from anywhere."

"Anywhere?" Haven asked, intrigued. Now this could be fun.

"Anywhere," Natasha answered, waggling her eyebrows. "Now, I will say, getting the fit right can be a little funny, since you do have to get the vibe in there and situated just right, so sometimes you need to go up a size or two. Why don't you go try these on, and I'll help your boyfriend here download the app."

"You can do that? The trying on, I mean."

"Sure can. Just like swimsuits at the mall; do it over your regular underwear. And while you're in there, I can also maybe help him pick out a couple of other things you two might like. Sound like a plan?"

It sounded like a damn good plan as far as Haven was concerned. A thrill shot through her, taking the items from Natasha. Turning to look at Elliot, she hoped that he was still okay with all of this. He'd been referred to as "boyfriend" twice in a matter of minutes, and hadn't bothered issuing a correction. Haven didn't know if that was out of embarrassment or because he liked hearing it as much as she did. Or maybe he just hadn't felt it was worth the effort.

Elliot winked, nodding his head back toward the dressing rooms in the corner, a massive smile on his face. His real smile. The one she knew he only busted out when he was comfortable and happy. It sent even more excitement rushing through her.

"Okay then. Just behave yourself while I'm gone." She returned his wink, her cheeks starting to heat up.

"I absolutely will not."

Oh, fuck...

CHAPTER SIX

A LOUD THUMP echoed through the dimly lit dressing room, greeting Elliot as he walked in. His hands were full, armed with an array of items that Natasha had suggested, including a few that were designed for couples. He didn't have the heart to tell her that he and Haven weren't a real couple and that he was only along for the ride. He'd enjoyed hearing her refer to him as "boyfriend." Enjoyed it even more when Haven hadn't corrected her either, allowing him to continue to pretend like that's exactly what he was.

"Fudgesicles!"

Haven's sweet voice rang out, acting as a homing device, drawing him to her. Even when she was cursing, there was a happiness to her voice that somehow penetrated everything. It was part of what made her so irresistible.

"You okay in there?" he asked, leaning against the dressing stall. The dark-green curtain was drawn, keeping her out of view, fueling his already wild thoughts about what was going on in there. Natasha had downloaded the app for the vibrating panties to his phone, showing him all the different settings, before loading him up—concentrating on one particular item—and sending him back here.

"It's one of our most popular toys. Great for beginners, couples, you name it," she said with a wink as she pushed him in the direction of the dressing room. "Don't be afraid to take it for a test drive."

The woman had no idea just how badly he wanted to do just that. She also had no idea how bad an idea that was. Kissing Haven last night was...everything. It had been an item on his own naughty list for damn near a decade, ever since he'd come home from his freshman year in college to find sixteen-year-old Haven and her friends hanging out by the pool in bikinis. Something had changed in the months since Christmas when he'd seen her last. Suddenly, she wasn't a little sister anymore. She was the kind of girl that one noticed from across the room, her smile lighting up the whole place. Topping it all off, she was still Haven—bubbly, happy, and so full of life that it seemed as if she could burst.

As much as he loved kissing her and couldn't wait to do it again, it wasn't lost on him that this was only temporary. She was using him to scratch an itch—to put a tick mark next to an item on her list. That was why he hadn't brought up the sex part of this deal. He wanted nothing more than to hold her in his arms, buried inside her as she fell apart. He also knew that it was going to ruin him. He wasn't a one-night stand kind of guy. Especially not with the girl he'd been fantasizing about for years. One kiss hadn't been enough; what made him think one night would be? But at the end of it, she was going to walk away, happy that she could say she had done it. As much as that was going to hurt, if it made her happy, he was more than willing to deal it with.

And pretend like it never happened, so that Hudson didn't kick his ass.

"Fine...I think," Haven answered from behind the curtain. "You think?"

"Yeah, I just can't..." she trailed off. The dark-green curtain swished open, revealing Haven, in nothing but her candy cane T-shirt and the panties, a defeated look on her face. "I don't think I'm getting the vibe part placed right. I dunno." Throwing her hands up in defeat, she stepped back into the stall, not bothering to close the curtain behind her. "I know I look too sexy for words right now, the whole two pair of panties thing."

Problem was, she did look too sexy for words. One look and he was instantly hard, fighting back a groan. The black lace pair Natasha had handed her were cut high, cupping her perfect ass in a way that made Elliot's mouth water. That wasn't what got him though. It was what was underneath those.

A pink polka dot thong.

Fuuuuuuuck...

"You look pretty damn good to me."

"Thanks." She blushed. Fuck, was she cute. "Help me get this thing placed right?"

Stepping inside, he redrew the curtain and dumped everything in his arms on the bench. The urge to kiss Haven rose in him again as he turned to look at her, her brown eyes shimmering in the low light. Holding back might just be the toughest thing he'd ever done.

"What makes you think it's not in there right?"

"I dunno, it just feels off."

Elliot pulled out his phone and opened the app, an impish grin tugging at his lips. He tried to hide it, not wanting to give Haven any indication of how excited he was. He needed to play this cool. If she was unfazed by the whole thing, then so was he. Scrolling through the settings for the vibe, it didn't take him long to decide which one to start with. No need to jack it up high, at least not yet.

Haven let out a squeak, jumping slightly. Elliot trusted that was from the toy, since he couldn't hear anything. Good to know it was discreet.

"How about now?"

"B-b-better."

"Yeah?" he asked, closing the small distance between them. There was a pull between them that he'd never felt, like two magnets, unable to resist each other. He wanted to make her feel more than *better*. He wanted to see what this thing could really do. So that every time she wore them from here on out, it was him she was thinking of. Haven inhaled sharply, her eyes pinned on his. "Does that feel good against your clit?"

Haven nodded, licking her lips. Elliot could see the pleasure building in her eyes, her features softening with each passing second. Wrapping his arm around her, hand planted firmly on the small of her back, he tapped the button on his phone, turning the vibrator up. A faint hum filled the air, only for a second, quickly covered up by Haven's whimper. A whimper that made his dick even harder. A whimper he wanted to turn into a scream.

"And now? Still sitting pretty?"

"Yea...yes..." Her voice was breathy, barely audible over the gasp that followed. That was all he needed to set him off.

A switch flipped inside him, his desire taking control. He couldn't hold back anymore. Haven wanted to be naughty? Then they were going to be naughty. He was in control now, and was about to give her exactly what she wanted. Leaning in, he placed his lips right up against her ear. "Tell me about it."

"Tell...tell you what?"

"How it feels against your pussy. What the rest of you is feeling. How badly you want to come. I want to know it all. Talk dirty to me, Haven, and don't hold back."

"It...feels good," she murmured, swallowing hard. Elliot felt her tense up in his arms before letting out a long, hard breath. "The vibrations against my clit...sending waves to the rest of my..."—she paused, sucking in another long breath—" my pussy. All of it...feels...faaaa..."

Her hands flew to his biceps, fingers digging into his muscles as her knees wobbled. Elliot tightened his hold on her. Reaching into his pocket, he dialed down the vibrations, wanting to drag this out. His time with her was limited, and he was going to make the most of it.

"And the rest of you?"

Haven mewled, pushing herself against him. His dick twitched, loving how her softness melded to him. Her eyes fluttered closed, her lips parted slightly. She was lost in her own world.

"Tell me, Haven," he prompted. "I want to know it all."

"I...I can't..."

"But you can." Haven shook her head, fingers digging into him more. "Want to know what I see?"

Haven nodded, eyes slowly opening, looking deep into his.

"I see a sexy little brunette, all hot and bothered. Hard nipples pushing against her bra, her sweet little pussy all wet and wanting more," he whispered, a roughness to his voice. Haven moaned in agreement, nodding furiously, her bottom lip caught between her teeth. It was a simple move, maybe even a subconscious one, but it all but made him come right there. "Fuck, Haven. If you had any idea what you do to me. Do you know how fucking hot it is to watch you like this?"

Haven shook her head, her breathing picking up speed. His naughty girl liked dirty talk. Noted.

Elliot shifted his hips, grinding against her, his erection bumping against the vibrator in the crotch of the panties. The buzz felt good against his hard-on, but not as good as she did. Haven's eyes went wide, the realization hitting her that he was just as turned on as she was.

"Tell me, naughty girl…do you want to come?"

Haven nodded.

"Use your words. Tell me what you want."

"I-I-I want to come. I want you to make me come…"

Her admission was music to his ears. No, it was more than that. It was the hottest, most erotic thing he'd ever experienced. Those words were going to be the soundtrack to every fantasy he had from here on out. This moment was real though. It wasn't just in his head. And he was going to enjoy every last millisecond of it.

Haven had laid a challenge at his feet. She wanted him to make her come. So that's exactly what he was going to do. And she was going to come harder than she ever had before.

Reaching back into his pocket, he grabbed his phone, dialing down the vibrator. He had bigger plans. Haven let out a disappointed noise, a cross between a whimper and a moan, making Elliot's insides twist a little. She wouldn't feel that way for long though, not if he did his job correctly.

"Don't worry, beautiful, I'm going to let you come. Just not yet."

Running his hands down over her ass, he gave it a squeeze, enjoying the feel of it in his palms. Looping his thumbs into the sides of both sets of panties, he quickly worked them down her legs. Haven wiggled her hips, simultaneously helping him and driving him wild. Reaching behind his back with one hand, he grabbed the first toy that he landed on, while scooping up that pink polka dot thong with his other. The little scrap of fabric was soaking wet, coating his fingers with her arousal. He let out a groan, loving the knowledge that he did that to her. Rising to his feet, he shoved them in his pocket, a keepsake for later.

"D," Haven said.

"I'm right here," he answered, dragging a hand along her wetness. Lifting his fingers to his mouth, he took a long, hard lick, enjoying the tanginess. Haven gasped. This was a side of him she'd never seen—a side very few people even knew existed—and he was having way more fun than he should showing it off.

Tightening his arm around her again, he captured her mouth in a punishing kiss. All this time he'd been teasing her, keeping her on the edge. But he needed her to know that this was more than just teasing. That kissing her last night wasn't a mistake, and that he was in this one hundred percent. No matter how casual and temporary it might be.

Clicking on the new toy, he slipped it between her legs. It was long, curved, and a pretty pink color that had Haven written all over it. The Cat's Meow was what Natasha had called it, and for the life of him Elliot couldn't figure out where these names came from. Although, as long as it did what he needed it to do, it probably didn't matter.

"Faaaaa," Haven called out, her voice long past the whispers she'd been keeping it to. If there had been any question about what they were up to in here, there wasn't anymore.

"My naughty girl likes that, huh?"

"Mmmm-hmmm."

"What if I just…" he trailed off, adjusting the toy slightly, moving it off her clit, parting her pussy lips. Haven circled her hips, her breath turning heavy as he moved it back and forth, trying to get it to where she wanted it. Each time he changed the angle, she let out a noise, similar to a purr, letting him know he was on to something.

So that's where the name comes from…

"Please, please," Haven cried, her body shaking. Elliot could tell she was close, and he couldn't wait to see what happened next.

"Please what, beautiful?"

"Please…make me come…please, I-I need to."

Elliot didn't need to hear any more. Her plea sparked something inside him, turning his own lust-fueled desire to push her over the edge up to eleven. His whole body was on fire, his mind focused on one thing and one thing only. Making Haven Taylor explode.

Clicking the little button on the vibrator, he switched the pattern, slipping it inside her. She was wet from all his efforts, making the process easier than expected. Slowly working it in and out of her, his thumb found her clit, circling it. Haven howled, a string of muffled curses following the primal noise. Knees wobbling, she clutched onto him harder, burying her face in the crook of his neck.

Elliot watched as her orgasm ripped through her, soaking in the moment—her warm breath through his T-shirt, her nails digging into his skin, her wetness covering his hand as he continued, not letting up until he knew she was done. He was committing it all to memory, and his heart soared.

A few moments later, Haven looked up at him, eyes glassy, skin flushed, a new glow to her. A glow that he was responsible for. His heart skipped a beat, her beauty almost overwhelming. Regular Haven was already too much, but postorgasm Haven? Fuck, there was no better sight. He was a goner. There would be no recovering from this.

"Holy smokes."

Slowly loosening her grip on his arms, Haven eased herself back from him. Instantly missing her against him, the sensation jolted him back to reality. He'd just gotten Haven off, with a sex toy, in public. Holy smokes was right.

Still, he wanted more. His dick was aching, straining against his zipper, his tongue dying for more of a taste of her. Lowering his head, he kissed her softly, a reminder that this wasn't over.

"Just wait until you see what I can do when I actually touch you."

CHAPTER SEVEN

HAVEN EXAMINED her reflection in the mirror, unable to hold back her smile. The off-the-shoulder, A-line green satin dress reminded her of the one that Hollie Berry had worn in *Chasing Snowflakes*—the diagonal pleating across the bust on Haven's, where Hollie's was smooth, the only major difference—and filled Haven with a new confidence. Excitement over the perfection of the dress brewed within her, threatening to explode at any moment.

Then again, maybe it wasn't the dress she was so excited about.

It had only been a few hours since she and Elliot had parted ways, each returning to their respective homes to prep and change for the Atlanta Rising Christmas Party. Haven's to-do list also included packing for Christmas break, since she planned on spending the next couple of nights at Elliot's. Her original plan had been to only spend Sunday night there, easing the early morning rush for the flight back to Boise the next day, but now that pole-dancing lessons were on the docket, the plan had to be shifted.

Oh yeah, and that other item they were checking off the list tonight.

A shiver ran up Haven's spine, memories of earlier in the dressing room at Tingles flashing back. Her whole body was consumed, recalling the incredible amount of pleasure she had felt—a level of intensity she hadn't realized was possible. That was, until D.B. Elliot and his insanely dirty mouth.

Had he always been such a dirty talker? Haven never would have expected that from Elliot, but then again, there was that expression for a reason. *It's always the quiet ones.* Either way, she fucking loved it. His words alone had lit her up like the Christmas tree in Times Square. Add in all those fancy moves with that vibrator, and she'd been toast. The whole experience had removed any and all reservations about their extracurriculars tonight. Instead, it had left her hoping that the take-charge, bossy side of him she'd witnessed in the dressing room was going to make another appearance.

The only problem was, she already knew she wanted more than just tonight.

Something had changed over the last two days that Haven couldn't name. Elliot had gone from bonus big brother and trusted friend to…more. And that wasn't just because he'd made her lose her mind in a sex shop. The thought of being near him made her insides turn to mush. She was looking forward to this Christmas party for the chance to hold his hand, to be close to him as they danced. Letting her mind wander, she liked the idea of that never ending. Of spending nights on the couch together, going out and trying new restaurants. Of her sitting in the WAGS section at Atlanta Rising games as an actual WAG. The knowledge that after they traveled back to Boise for Christmas this all would be over made her nauseous.

"You look like a present that is just asking to be

unwrapped."

Haven jumped at the sound of Elliot's voice. Twirling around, she found him leaning against the doorjamb, looking dapper in his custom-cut suit. He must have let himself in, that spare key she'd made him "just in case" going to good use. Her heart called out to him at the same time her lady bits tingled, thinking about what was under the crisp white button-down. Stepping into the room, Elliot slipped an arm around her waist, kissing her softly.

Don't stop, don't stop...

Elliot didn't seem to get her telepathic message though and gently released her, letting his eyes dance up and down her body.

"Thanks. It's just like Hollie Berry's in—"

"*Chasing Snowflakes,*" he answered, cutting her off. "I know the movie well. Someone has made me sit through it like a million times."

"It's a cinematic classic, thank you."

"We'll have to agree to disagree on that one." He laughed. "Ready?"

Haven nodded. She was more than ready.

Thirty minutes later, stuff all packed in the back of Elliot's car, they were walking into the ballroom at Archer's Green, Atlanta's premier—and very exclusive—country club. Haven had been here only once before—for the wedding reception of Elliot's coach, Gunnar Gracin, and the team's owner, Felicity Sutherland, over the summer. That had been a magical evening, hanging out with Elliot and all his team-mates, laughing and dancing. She could only hope that tonight was just as amazing.

Given the way he was looking at her, she was confident that it would be.

Every inch of the ballroom was covered in Christmas decorations, giving it a warm and welcoming feel. A buffet was off to their right—a long line of players making their way through, loading up their plates—and a bar to their left. Elliot placed his hand on the small of her back, the heat from it catching her off guard, but in a good way. She hadn't realized that she was missing such a feeling, but now that it was there, she didn't want it to disappear.

"Elliot!" Chance Walker, another midfielder for the Atlanta Rising and Elliot's best friend on the team, called out, arms raised high in the air, as if seeing the two of them walk in was a massive surprise. "And the lovely Miss Haven."

Taking her hand, Chance lightly kissed her knuckles. Haven tittered softly, loving how goofy he was. She liked all Dobby's teammates on the Rising, which was more than she could say for teams he'd played for in the past. Usually there was at least one guy who was nothing more than a complete jackass and always managed to ruin things. Not with this crowd. The dynamic the whole group had was great, both on and off the field. Elliot's smaller circle—which included Chance, as well as striker Dash Lazaro and goalkeeper Liam Daley, not to mention the newest addition to their group, midfielder Mahoney Holmes—was as close as they came. Haven knew they were the kind of friends you had for life, no matter if one of them was traded or retired.

"Where's Delaney?" Haven asked, looking around for Chance's fiancée.

"She, Avery, and Talia are on a pilgrimage to the bathroom. The first of many tonight, I'm sure," he told her, already answering her follow-up question about Liam's and Dash's girlfriends.

A wave of self-consciousness hit her. She was looking forward to seeing the girls, who had always been very accepting of her as part of the group. But at an event like this, it was hard to ignore the fact that she was the only nonsignificant other. Everyone else was paired off, and she was just here as a friend. And maybe not even that. She was the little sister of his friend. In her mind, she and Elliot had always had their own friendship, separate from Hudson, but suddenly, her own insecurities were getting the best of her.

What if that wasn't really the case? What if everything leading up to this moment was just him being a good friend to Hudson and watching out for his little sister? No, that couldn't be. One did not go streaking with someone you weren't friends with. And one most certainly didn't treat little sisters to world-shattering, semipublic orgasms. Those were what you *stopped* guys from doing to your little sister. She was being ridiculous. Just because she wanted more of those orgasms—more of Elliot in general—didn't mean she needed to let it rule her thoughts. Tonight was no different from any other time they'd hung out with his friends and their partners.

"I missed the first bathroom trip of the night? Darn it!" she exclaimed, trying to play off her anxiety. Elliot's arm tightened around her, as if he could tell something was off. She couldn't let him know though. She wasn't ready to admit to anything. Not that there was anything to admit to. A stupid little fleeting crush was not a conversation they would be having.

"Don't worry, you didn't," Delaney interjected, sliding up to Haven, greeting her with a hug. "Avery tripped in her shoes, so we ran to the front desk to see if they had a Band-Aid."

"I'm usually so good at walking in these," Avery, a petite redhead with a thick southern drawl, added. "But Liam was walking fast, and with those crazy long legs of his, I couldn't keep up and—"

"Do not blame me," Liam said, his Irish accent just as strong as Avery's southern one. "You know how I feel about those shoes."

"You love them!"

"It was like watching a chihuahua walk with a great Dane. She takes sixteen of her steps for every one of his," Talia explained as she laughed.

Haven giggled, watching Avery scowl at her roommate's comment. They all knew it was true—Liam was the tallest on the team at six feet, five inches, while Avery, the team's physical therapist, was more than a foot shorter than he was. They were an undeniably cute couple though, and a pang of jealousy sliced through Haven again.

"But I was promised food after the Band-Aid, so, buffet now, before we all regret our life choices," Talia commanded, pointing to the line. She wasted no time in turning on her heel and heading that way, Delaney and Avery right behind her.

"Haven, you coming?" Avery asked, stopping after a few steps and looking back at her.

Haven looked to Elliot, not sure what the plan was. Normally she wouldn't have hesitated to automatically join the ladies, but for some reason, she was frozen in place. She didn't need Elliot's permission, but something inside her wanted reassurance that he would be right there waiting for her.

Elliot winked at her. "You have fun with the girls; I'm going to grab a drink." Leaning down, he placed a soft kiss on her forehead, butterflies erupting inside her with the contact. "Just don't gossip too much about me. I'd hate to have to spank you later," he whispered into her ear. Shivers ran down her spine, releasing her own sass.

"Don't threaten me with a good time, Daubney Blake."

OMG, who am I?!

Returning his wink from a moment ago, she scampered off to join the rest of the group, feeling rather proud of herself. She was doing this. She was claiming her coal.

CHAPTER EIGHT

"I saw that," Chance said, not bothering to lower his voice. Elliot had half expected there to be a singsongy, know-it-all tone to it, but thankfully that didn't make an appearance.

"Saw what?" he asked, giving his buddy a slight shrug, turning to head to the bar.

He knew better than to try and play it off. These guys had been giving him a hard time about Haven since they'd first met her back at Dash's birthday party in the spring. They'd seen right through him and his line about how she was "just his best friend's little sister". Not that their X-ray vision had stopped him from trying to keep up the ruse. At some point though, he was going to have to come clean, let these guys in on his not-so-secret. Maybe now was that point.

"You know what."

Elliot leaned against the bar, turning to his buddies, trying to figure out exactly where to start. Something had changed between him and Haven in the last couple days—there was no doubt about that. He just wasn't sure how much of that change he was really willing to share. Or how much of it was one-sided. He knew these guys would gladly listen to him, help him work out his thoughts on the matter, but he still wasn't sure. It wasn't the part about being emotionally vulnerable that stopped him—these were his teammates, and they knew each other well enough that they would never judge him for that. Each one of them had gone through their own moment when it came to their relationships, and the rest of the group had been there to offer support. It was what they did for each other. And this would be no different. Wasn't this what he'd just bitched at Mahoney about? Not trusting the group? Yeah, it was time to come clean.

If he could only figure out what to say.

"You kissed her," Dash said, his South American accent making those three words sound a lot racier than they were.

"I did."

"What happened to 'I am not into my best friend's sister'?" Mahoney asked, arm wrapped around his boyfriend, Trent. The two looked like they just stepped out of a menswear catalog in matching suits and coordinating ties, bright smiles on their faces.

"We all knew it was a lie, but are you finally ready to admit that?" Dash followed up.

Elliot sighed. Turning to the bartender, he ordered a beer for himself and champagne for Haven, letting the question settle. He could feel five sets of eyes trained on him, waiting on an answer.

"I am."

"Fuck!" Liam exclaimed, his deep voice edging out Chance's "Yes!"

"What? I'm admitting it. You guys have been giving me shit for months and now you're upset that I'm owning up to it?"

"No," Liam answered. "We're thrilled you are owning up to it. But now I owe Chance fifty bucks."

"You had a bet going?"

Of course they fucking did. Elliot shook his head, taking a long drag of his beer. He didn't know why he was surprised.

"I said you'd have it figured out by Christmas, Liam thought New Year's was the trick. Dash said it would be well into next year. Mahoney stayed out of it," Chance explained.

"Not my place to judge. Not after how long I kept my secret," Mahoney said.

"Talia backed me up," Dash defended, grabbing his own drink order. "Said that her conversations with Haven supported the 'nothing but my brother's best friend' deal. I thought I was safe."

"If it makes you feel better," Trent added. "I would have also said next season."

"So…what changed?" Chance asked, prodding like an old lady sitting in a rocking chair, waiting on all the latest gossip.

"It's complicated," Elliot answered, following the group back to their table. He didn't think it was really his place to tell the guys all about Haven's naughty list, but he figured he could at least dance around it.

"More complicated than being into a girl who is crushing on your teammate?" Liam asked.

"Or pretending to be engaged to your best friend?" Chance followed up.

"Or keeping your relationship secret because she is the daughter of the coach? And he is already pissed at you for something you did not do?" Dash threw in.

"Or hiding your sexuality *and* your boyfriend until you're unwillingly outed?" Mahoney added.

Touché…

His buddies all looked at him expectantly. They knew complicated. Their relationships hadn't been simple and straightforward either. Letting out a huff, Elliot sat back in his chair.

"I love her. We all know it. And I have loved her for a long fucking time, okay?" he acquiesced. The guys all nodded, waiting for him to continue. "And these last few days, we've gotten closer. Really fucking *close*. I can't tell you why without betraying her trust. Right now, all I can do is hope that maybe she's starting to see me as more than Hudson's best friend. Because God knows, she's been more than just his sister for…"

"We got you," Chance said jumping in where he trailed off.

"What can we do to help?" Liam asked.

Elliot thought for a moment. There wasn't anything he could think of that these guys could do. He loved knowing that they were willing though. For as much shit as they had given him over this, each one of them was ready and willing to do whatever it took to make sure he got his lady. Too bad he still wasn't sure that Haven had any real interest in him past this list.

His thoughts were interrupted by a squeal, heard loud and clear over the pop tune the DJ was playing. Turning around, he saw their women heading this way, led by Delaney, the look on her face letting them all know that she was up to no good. Eyes darting over to Haven, he found an equally guilty expression on her face. Oh boy.

"We're going pole dancing!" Delaney announced, sliding a plate of food in front of Chance.

Elliot choked on his beer, holding in his laugh, as Chance looked at his fiancée like she had lost her mind. It was a look he understood, better than his teammate realized. It was the same one he'd given Haven the night before, just before she'd kissed him.

"I did not hear you properly," Chance responded.

"You did. We're going pole dancing."

"Now?"

"No, tomorrow."

"Nothing about that sounds like a good idea," Liam muttered.

"Yeah, you can count us out of that one," Trent commented, taking a swig of his beer.

"Haven was telling us all about it! Apparently there are lessons at the Fox Den and she and Elliot are going tomorrow, and we said we'd join!" Avery added.

All the guys turned and looked at Elliot as one, almost as if it had been a coordinated move in a play. Each had the same look on their face—confusion mixed with amusement. It was perfectly clear they were all just waiting for him to tap dance his way out of this one.

So much for keeping Haven's list to themselves...

"I told you, it's complicated." He shrugged. There, that would hopefully pacify them.

Looking over to Haven, he reached for her hand, tugging her closer to him. She mouthed "sorry" to him, eyes darting away from his, her cheeks turning pink. He had no idea what she was apologizing for though. Turning in his chair, he tilted his head, trying to meet her gaze. When he finally found it, his heart squeezed—her soft brown eyes were full of emotion.

"It just slipped out," she whispered. "I didn't mean to turn it into a thing."

"It's fine."

"I didn't mean to embarrass you in front of the guys."

That's what she was concerned about? Well, fuck. There was no way he was going to let her worry about something as stupid as that.

"You didn't. I don't care what they think about it. I only care that you're happy."

Haven's cheeks flushed even more, and Elliot's insides turned into lava. She was so fucking cute. No, she was more than that. Haven Taylor was sexy. Watching her these last few days as she embraced a new side to herself had been unreal—an honor he would never forget. Even in the awkward moments, like sitting in that strip club, he'd enjoyed every second. He wasn't sure anything would ever top the experience they'd shared this morning at Tingles. She'd been putty in his hands, the look of ecstasy on her face seared into his memory. He wanted to experience that over and over again—taking her to new heights and showing her things that no one else could.

If only it would last longer than this weekend.

"You are happy with how things are going, yes?" he asked, wanting to make sure he wasn't making assumptions.

"You have no idea."

"Oh, I think I do." Sliding his hand to the small of her back, he drew her in closer, in between his open legs. She was only slightly taller than he was in this position, their bodies all but touching. He crooked his finger, telling her to come closer. A coy smile tugged at her lips as she complied, leaning in close enough for him to whisper. "I can still hear your moans from the dressing room. And I can't wait to hear them again later."

Haven's audible gasp was enough to send a bolt of lust straight through Elliot, making his dick twitch. The rest of the group continued to chatter, their words fading into the beat from the dance hit playing. The only things that existed right now were Haven and the pounding of his own heart. No other woman had ever had this kind of effect on him. She was the only one who could make everything else melt away with a smile, a look, or even a sigh. It didn't matter that a moment ago he'd been wondering if Haven could ever feel the same about him as he did her. If she walked away from him without a second look when they got back home, he'd find a way to deal with it. At least he had this moment.

The heavy beat of the music faded, melding into something soft and slow. It was a tune he recognized but didn't know the name of—one that was perfect for holding someone close and getting lost in them. Which was exactly what he wanted to do.

Without another word, he pushed to his feet, grabbing Haven's hand and leading her to the dance floor. For a split second he felt bad for leaving his buddies behind, not even acknowledging them, but that feeling disappeared when he saw the rest of them follow suit. A blink of an eye later, Haven's arms were around his neck, her body pressed against his. She settled into his arms, like a cat nesting in a warm blanket. Sliding his hand down her back, he let it rest just above her ass, wanting so badly to give it a squeeze. He could still feel it in his palm, how perfectly it had fit there. Instead, he changed his rhythm, slowing down their movements. Haven followed along, letting him guide her, and once again, the rest of the room melted away. As long as she was in his arms, he was the king of the world.

"Dobby…" Haven whispered.

Elliot responded by leaning down, resting his forehead against hers. She relaxed even more in his arms, letting him know he was onto something. She was just as lost in this moment as he was. He rolled his hips, closing the impossibly small gap between them, creating a friction that was electric. His dick was rock-hard, and there was no way she couldn't feel it. Still, she met his movements with those of her own, upping the ante and the friction.

Her lips were millimeters from his, so close that her breath tickled his lips as she exhaled. Elliot fought off the urge to kiss her, reminding himself this wasn't the time or place. The kiss to the forehead earlier was one thing—calm, cool, controlled. He was going to be none of those things right now with everything he was feeling.

Haven shifted in his arms, letting out a low moan as she halfway ground against his erection. The sound was music to his ears, his body responding the only way it knew how. There was no resisting anymore.

Elliot's mouth crashed down on Haven's, capturing it in a punishing kiss. She kissed him back with just as much passion, her tongue finding his almost instantly. If he'd thought that he was on fire before, it was only because he'd never experienced anything like the inferno that was raging through him now. Every inch of him was turned on. This wasn't just a kiss. This was everything he'd ever felt about her—everything he'd ever wanted to say but hadn't. All the years of holding back, of lying to himself about how he felt about Haven, brought to life.

He continued to kiss her like his life depended on it, not wanting this feeling to end. It had to; he knew that. Eventually the song would end, or someone would call them out for making out on the dance floor. If he was lucky, it would be one of the guys and not his coach. But even if it was Gunnar, he had no regrets. Except maybe not manning up sooner.

"You are really good at that," Haven murmured, coming up for air as the song ended.

"I'm good at a lot of things," he replied, unable to hold back his smirk.

"Sorry to interrupt," Dash said, magically appearing at their side, waving his hand for attention. "Felicity wants a team photo. Now. And she scares me, so, let us go."

"Your future mother-in-law scares you?" Elliot quipped, unable to help himself at the easy jab. When Dash had set his sights on Talia, they'd all known he was messing with fire, hitting on the coach's daughter. But when Gunnar married Felicity, the team's owner, things got that much more complicated for him. Everything worked out in the end, but they never passed on an opportunity to rag him about it.

"And your future brother-in-law does not scare you on some level?"

Brother-in-law.

The term hit Elliot like a ton of bricks. He hadn't done much thinking about Hudson these last few days—not near as much as he should have. Your best friend was not exactly who you were thinking about as you're fucking his sister with a vibrator. If Hudson knew what he'd done...no, Elliot wasn't going there. Haven was his focus right now; he could deal with Hudson later.

Or never. Since they were not going to tell him about their arrangement.

"Be right back," he told Haven, rushing off with Dash.

Fifteen minutes later they were done. Elliot rushed back to Haven, with Liam, Dash, Mahoney, and Chance hot on his heels, just as excited to get back to their own partners. They found them all walking back up the spiral staircase from the bathroom, the lot of them in a fit of giggles about something. Elliot desperately wanted to get back to the moment they were having on the dance floor, but it was lost. Instead, he would settle for the sound of her beautiful laughter.

"It got chilly," Haven said, pulling her black wool wrap tighter around her body.

The wind whipped through the covered portion of the Archer's Green entrance, Haven shivering as it hit her bare legs. Elliot said a silent plea for the valet to hurry up. He was normally a fairly patient guy, but he was dying to get Haven home. More dancing and plenty of laughter had made the rest of the evening fly by, but had done little to ease the hard-on raging in his pants. If anything, it had only made it worse. The sultry looks Haven had been giving him also threw gas onto an already out-of-control fire. He wondered if she had any idea what she was doing, or if it was all subconscious.

"Don't worry, as soon as we get home, the only things you're going to be are hot and bothered."

"Promises, promises," she tutted.

Elliot flexed his hand, trying to stop himself from giving her backside a little swat. There would be time for that later. Instead, he started to step in closer.

"Here you go, sir," the valet said, cutting off his stride.

Fuck...

Elliot took the keys from the guy and handed him a tip. Turning back to Haven, he smiled, his whole body feeling full with the knowledge that at least for tonight, she belonged to him. Spinning around to face him, Haven smiled, right as another gust of wind blew through the tunnel. Haven froze in place, the wind continuing to carry her skirt. Much like Marilyn Monroe standing on top of the grate, the fabric billowed outward, showing off exactly what Haven had on underneath her dress.

Nothing.

Rushing over to her, Elliot smoothed out her skirt, his cock throbbing with anticipation. "Haven Mae Taylor," he scolded in a low voice, ushering her to her side of the car. "Are you not wearing underwear?"

"Go commando was on the list."

Elliot let out a groan. He was already painfully hard; now he wasn't sure he was going to make it home. Opening the door, he helped her into the car. He needed to get her home. Now.

"Is that a problem?" she asked, turning to him in the driver's seat.

"Not at all." He took her hand, placing it on the bulge in his pants. Haven's eyes went wide, her fingers gripping him through the fabric. "I just very much need to get you home, so I can show you exactly what being naughty earns you."

CHAPTER NINE

FOR THE FIRST time in her life, Haven understood exactly what it meant for her body to vibrate. And it had nothing to do with the Cat's Meow that had come home with her from Tingles earlier.

No, this was pure D.B. Elliot.

It was a mix of nerves and anticipation that was coursing through her, making the goose bumps climb up her skin. The knowledge of what was about to go down was both empowering and paralyzing, keeping her frozen in place just inside Elliot's front door. She needed to act—to do *something*—she just wasn't sure what.

Get it together, girl, you're supposed to be claiming your coal...

Whipping around, she watched Elliot lock the door behind him and then shrug out of his jacket. She could see his muscles rippling under his dress shirt, and her mouth watered at the thought of running her hands along them. A shirtless Elliot wasn't something new—hell, they'd been naked together the other night while streaking—but this time, there was more to it. She was dying to touch him all over, to learn what his skin felt like against hers. It was now or never.

Haven lunged toward Elliot, grabbing hold of his shoulders as he turned to face her, kissing him hard. There was a soft thud as their bodies collided, none of her usual grace making an appearance in this moment. Trying to deepen the kiss, Haven was all thumbs, fumbling about, unable to get ahold of him quite the way she wanted. She could only imagine how ridiculous she looked, because if it was even a fraction of what she was feeling, she wouldn't blame Elliot for backing out of their agreement right here and now.

Elliot seemed to understand what she was trying to accomplish though. In one swift move he captured her hands in his and spun her around, pressing her back to the front door, pinning her arms above her head. How he'd done that, she had no idea. Her head was too busy getting lost in the kiss he was now controlling, his strong lips slowly guiding hers in what felt like a symphony. The coolness of the door through her dress was a sharp contrast to the heat that was crawling up her skin, as Elliot ground his hips against hers, that glorious bulge still front and center.

"Hey there, naughty girl," Elliot growled. His hips pressed against her again, drawing a moan from her. How was it that just a bulge felt that damn good? "Slow down. No need to rush."

Haven nodded furiously, her breath heavy and lust-filled. Pinned against the door like this, she felt so open and exposed, yet so turned on she didn't know where to start. She'd never felt like this, so full of desire that it fueled her every move. No one had the power over her that Elliot did.

"Now, there are a couple of ways we can do this," he continued, his eyes darkening, filling with the same lust she was feeling. "You can continue to maul me like a baby tiger, or…" He paused, swallowing hard. Haven watched as his Adam's apple bobbed in his throat, the simple, natural movement sending a zing straight between her legs. "You can let me have my way with you and show you exactly what it means to have your world rocked."

Oh, fuck…

Haven's breath caught in her throat, all of the air seemingly sucked right out of the room with Elliot's dirty words. She was never going to be able to look at him the same way after this, knowing exactly what that mouth was capable of. At least verbally. She could only imagine what else he had up his sleeve where that body part was concerned, much less other parts of him.

"Baby tigers are cute," she replied, her mind suddenly blank, unable to think of any other response.

"They are." Lowering his head, he nipped at her neck, his teeth lightly grazing the skin. More goose bumps covered her skin, making her shiver with each new nibble. "As are you, Haven. You are so fucking adorable, I can't stand it. You have no idea what you do to me."

"R-r-really?"

"Really." His deep voice had a new intensity to it, his pupils darkening even more. "And I don't care what anyone thinks; you're not a Goody Two-Shoes. Far from it, beautiful. You are my naughty girl."

Oh, fuck…

Heart squeezing, Haven tried to tamp down the swell of emotion rising in her. His naughty girl. *His.* That was what she wanted to be in this moment. His. Fuck, that's what she wanted in general. To be his. In whatever form that took.

"I'm yours," she repeated, her voice barely audible over the sound of her heart crashing against her ribcage. For a second she thought maybe he didn't hear her, until the knowing smirk spread across his face. "Have your way with me, Dobby. Please."

"Gladly."

Next thing Haven knew, Elliot had scooped her up, hands digging into her ass underneath her dress, walking them toward the bedroom. The bright lights from downtown Atlanta shone through the windows, giving off just enough light. Elliot continued to nibble at her neck, Haven letting out a small yelp when he found a particular spot that made her think she was going to come instantly. Hell, if he kept it up, she just might.

"Time to show me what else you're not wearing underneath this dress," he growled, lowering her to the ground.

His fingers found the zipper on the back of her dress, tugging it down. A quicky shimmy and it was in a pile at her feet, leaving her completely naked. It had been a bold choice to also forgo her bra, but the dress had been fitted enough that she felt she could get away with it. After all, if she was going commando, she might as well go all the way, right?

"Fuck me, you are incredible."

A blush crept up Haven's cheeks, a moment of bashfulness hitting her. It didn't last long though. A second later Elliot's mouth was on her breast, his tongue laving her nipple, while his fingers mirrored the attention on the other. The sensation sent her reeling, replacing anything she might have been feeling prior. There was nothing else to feel but *good* as he did this. No other thoughts were possible, other than concentrating on what Elliot was doing. Her whole body reacted, all the little hairs on her arms standing at attention.

Fuck, he hadn't been kidding when he'd told her to just wait until he actually touched her. He knew what he was doing. And this was just her nipples he was playing with. What was going to happen when he moved south?

Wetness pooled between her legs at the thought, her pussy aching for attention. She wanted to feel him there. Wanted to know if that talented tongue of his felt this amazing everywhere on her body. Wiggling her hips, she tried to make contact with his erection again, dying for that friction she'd felt earlier, realizing a little too late that physics weren't on her side here. There was no way to make the contact she was craving while they were standing. She needed to do something; she was desperate.

Reaching in between her legs, she slid her hand through her sex, letting her wetness cover her fingers. The contact felt good but still wasn't enough. She needed more. But before she could get her fingers to her clit, Elliot grabbed her wrist, yanking it away.

"Uh-uh, naughty girl," he scolded. "That's my pussy. Only I get to play with it. Understand me?"

Haven nodded, a whole new wave of desire crashing over her. Never in a million years would she have thought she would like this alpha thing Elliot had going on, but apparently she'd been wrong. She was putty in his hands, every inch of her charged and ready to go. Lifting her hand to his mouth, Elliot sucked on it, licking her arousal clean off her.

"You taste like honey." Yanking her in close, he kissed her hard. Legs wobbling more, she clutched him, not wanting to fall. "But here's the thing, beautiful. What you just did was very naughty. And I believe I told you earlier what happens to naughty girls."

"And I believe I told you not to threaten me with a good time," she sassed back. Where the response had come from, Haven wasn't sure. There was a new, sudden boldness flowing through her. Something about the taste of herself on his tongue had empowered her. She knew what was coming, and she couldn't wait.

Elliot let out a low, guttural noise. One that was so damn sexy it made her want to figure out more ways to misbehave just so he would make it again. Spinning her around, Elliot pushed her over the bed, leaving her ass in the air. His large hand ran over her cheek, as if he were smoothing out a blanket. Just as quickly as it had been there, it was gone, coolness replacing it.

Smack!

The hardness of his hand met her ass, causing her to cry out. To Haven's surprise though, it wasn't pain that followed —it was pleasure. Pleasure that radiated through her body, making her want more. So, so much more.

"Again," she cried. "Please."

"Again?" Elliot questioned. "My naughty girl wants another?"

"Please."

Smack!

His hand met her other side this time, sending the same wave of desire through her. All Haven could think was that it was a good thing she had the bed for support—there was no way her legs could support her now. She was almost a puddle. And she hadn't even come yet.

That was about to change though. A heartbeat later, Elliot's mouth was on her pussy, his tongue diving straight in. He was like a man possessed, sucking, nibbling, licking, not leaving a centimeter untouched. When he found her clit, circling it with his tongue, Haven screamed, unable to hold back. He was making her feel things she never thought possible. Things that she had only read about, convinced it was made up for books. Apparently, she'd been wrong.

Continuing to focus on her clit, his thumb quickly replacing his tongue, Elliot slipped two fingers inside her, tapping lightly on the spot he'd found earlier in the day. That was all it took. Whatever buildup Haven had been experiencing was over, all of it thundering down on her, pleasure skyrocketing though her. Every nerve ending came alive, firing all at once, her orgasm taking over her body.

"That's my girl," Elliot whispered in her ear, his fingers still working her through the last of her aftershocks.

"Oh…my…goodness…"

"I'm not done with you yet."

Wrapping his arms around her, Elliot lifted her and scooted her up the bed, laying her down on her back. Letting her eyes dance up and down his body, she realized he'd managed to get undressed without her noticing, his glorious naked form on display. His beautiful, thick cock was standing at attention, and her mouth watered all over again. She reached for it, surprised when Elliot didn't knock her hand away. He felt glorious in her hand, as she slowly stroked up and down. There was something missing though.

Swiping at her pussy, she covered her hand in her wetness again, swiftly returning to his shaft. Haven resumed her up and down movements, this time assisted by the results of the best orgasm she'd ever experienced.

"Oh, fuuuuuck, Haven," Elliot groaned, his voice strangled with his own pleasure. Still, he didn't stop her. Just closed his eyes, getting lost in the moment. Haven felt powerful, enjoying the control she suddenly had over him. She liked Elliot being in charge, but this was fun too.

Reaching for the nightstand, Elliot grabbed a condom, ripping it open and handing it to her. Stopping her movement, she sheathed him, her pulse kicking up a notch.

She was about to have sex with Elliot.

"You want my cock, baby?" he asked, lining himself up with her entrance.

"Please…"

Elliot sank in slowly, both of them letting out a groan as

he entered her. He felt sensational, filling her up and stretching her in a way no one else had. Once he was fully in, he paused as the both of them adjusted to each other. It was only a short moment, though, before Elliot drew back and repeated the movement again. Haven mewled, loving the feel of him inside her. He soon found his rhythm—quick hard thrust, followed by long slow one that Haven was sure he was doing just to tease her. Wrapping her legs around his waist, she met him thrust for thrust, searching for what she knew they were both after.

Long gone was the wild, frenzied, lust-fueled haze they had been in when they had first gotten home. Alpha Elliot was still here, but now his focus was on their connection. With their foreheads pressed together, his kisses were long and slow, like he was letting her in on a secret. This wasn't just sex. It was the two of them coming together, their life-long bond taking on a new form. The more he moved, the more Haven craved, but not just the amazing thing she was feeling physically. Her heart was craving more. She wanted to stay just like this, wrapped up in his arms, all his attention on her.

She knew it had to end though. The telltale feeling in her belly was growing stronger by the second, her second orgasm building like a tidal wave. Elliot must have sensed it as well, picking up his pace, pushing up to change his angle. He was hitting her in all the right spots now. A swipe of his thumb over her clit and that was that. Haven went flying, hurtling over the edge, her whole body going rigid as her pussy clamped down on Elliot's cock. He didn't let up though, speeding up even more, a primal look on his face and a loud roar escaping his lips as his own climax racked him.

Collapsing down onto her, Elliot moaned into her shoulder. His breath tickled her sensitive skin, the weight of him on top of her comforting. Like a warm blanket in the dead of winter, Haven never wanted to climb out from under him. Her heart was racing, every inch of her completely sated. World rocked indeed.

There was just one problem—one night wasn't ever going to be enough.

CHAPTER TEN

"I'm...I'm so excited!" Haven squealed, beaming up at Elliot. Her brown eyes sparkled, her smile ranging from ear to ear, as bright as he'd ever seen it.

"And you just can't hide it?" Talia quipped from the other side of Elliot.

"That's never been something I excelled at."

Elliot huffed out a laugh, loving her honesty. It was true; when Haven got excited about something, she was over the top about it. Something he was sure made her very endearing to the six-year-olds she spent her days with. Because if she could have found a way to actually bounce off the walls, Elliot was sure she would have. Which is why he was standing here now, a shiny silver pole in front of him.

The strip club in the light of day was still a little weird. Unnerving—maybe that was a better term. Without all the flashing lights, heavy beats, and the smoke machine, it almost looked like a regular bar. Just one with a stage. And poles.

Haven, Avery, Delaney, and Talia had been in giggles basically since the moment they all met up in the parking lot. Despite the cacophony the four of them created, Elliot could hear Haven's laughter loud and clear. It was music to his ears, a sound he knew he would never be able to get enough of. Hell, he was never going to be able to get enough of *her*.

Last night had been the best night of his life. There wasn't a single shred of doubt in his mind. Forget graduating, forget getting drafted, forget the first professional goal he'd ever scored. None of those moments compared with holding Haven in his arms while they danced. To having her on his arm as they hung out with his friends and teammates. To being the one whose name she had screamed as she came. He wanted more of that. Not just the orgasms—although he had a list of things as long as his arm that he wanted to do with her still. But all of it. Add in nights on the couch, weekends filled with running errands, and all the other day-to-day stuff that was forgotten about and taken for granted, and he couldn't think of a better life.

It simply wasn't going to be *his* life. At least not with Haven. If he was lucky, he would get to witness her share that with someone else. This weekend was a passing fling for her. A way for her to discover a new side to herself. He was just the means to an end.

"Y'all ready?" Jazzmin, their instructor for the afternoon, asked.

The tall Black woman was built like a gymnast, every inch of her solid muscle, with a power behind her stance that radiated off her. If it wasn't for the kind smile on her face, Elliot would have been intimidated. One look at her and it was clear she could take him and all three of the guys in a fight—at once. And win. Instead, she'd all but greeted them with a hug when they walked in, so excited to welcome them.

"I thought that maybe I was going to have to cancel, since it's the Sunday before Christmas! But look at the gift Santa just brought me!" she'd exclaimed. "Although y'all are gonna have to share, because we're only set up for four today."

Sure enough, four identical metal posts ran from floor to ceiling, screwed in on both ends, evenly spaced out on the stage. Each couple took a station, looking more like they were there for a workout than a striptease.

"Yes!" Avery replied, so enthusiastically that even Jazzmin was taken aback. "I already reminded everyone to stretch, since stretching is the most important thing you can do before any kind of physical activity."

Jazzmin looked at her quizzically, head tilted to the side, very obviously unsure what to do with the awkward little redhead. Elliot bit back a laugh. As the team PT, Avery was always after them to stretch. They were used to her reminders, but in the moment, he could see why such a thing came off strange.

"Just go with it," Talia told Jazzmin. "This is the least weird she's gonna be all day."

Jazzmin nodded, brows still furrowed, proceeding with her instructions. Leaning forward, Elliot wrapped his arms around Haven's waist, drawing her in close. She smelled like heaven—something light and airy that he couldn't name. No doubt his shower smelled the same way now, a fact he was sure to enjoy later.

"I'll help you stretch whatever you need," he whispered into her ear.

Haven giggled, squirming in his arms, her luscious ass rubbing up against the semi he was already sporting. She had made the same move multiple times last night in her sleep, curled up in his arms. He'd been all ready for round two, wanting to make the most of their one night together. After all, the agreement was one night—not one performance. That was, until he'd heard the soft snores and felt Haven's steady, even breath tickling his chest. The serene smile on her face melted his heart, and the only thing he wanted in that moment was to hold her for the rest of the night. So that was exactly what he did.

"I still feel your *stretching* from last night," she whispered back, an impish gleam in her eyes.

"Then I did something right."

"You sure did."

"Secrets don't make friends," Delaney teased, leaning over toward them.

"But friends make secrets," Haven sang back. "And Dobby is the best kind of friend."

Friend...she still thinks of me as just a friend...

"Dobby?" Chance repeated. "Like the house elf?"

Elliot nodded. He'd been preparing for this line of questioning for months, surprised that none of them had ever caught on to her calling him that.

"That's not why I call him that though. I've been calling him Dobby since I was two and he and my brother Hudson were five. I had a hard time saying Daubney and it came out Dobby, and then it just stuck."

"Hold on," Liam injected from his other side. "Your real name is Daubney?"

Elliot nodded again, holding out his hand as if to shake Liam's. "Daubney Blake Winston Elliot, at your service."

"Damn, that is a mouthful," Chance muttered.

"Wait, did they not know? OMG!" Haven said, spinning in his arms. "I can't believe I outed you like that. I'm so sorry."

"You can make it up to me with a kiss," he offered.

"Gladly."

Pushing to her tiptoes, Haven pressed her lips to his, lightly at first, her movements tentative. He couldn't let her get away with that though, tightening the arm he still had wrapped around her, deepening the kiss. The world seemed to stop, the rest of the club and everyone in it falling away.

Elliot wished they could stay like this forever, lost in one another, nowhere else to be except this moment.

"Just what the fuck are you doing?"

Haven pulled back from the kiss, a guilty look on her face as she glanced around trying to figure out the answer to the question. Elliot knew better though. The tone of Liam's voice was one she wouldn't know, but it was his Dash voice. The one he used only when he was confused by something their showoff of a teammate was doing.

"I am following the moves being demonstrated," Dash answered, eyes still focused on Jazzmin, as he bent around the pole, his ass sticking out. Talia stood behind him, hand clasped over her mouth. What Elliot wasn't sure of was if she was impressed or holding back laughter.

"Well done, Dash," Jazzmin said.

With a sashay of his hips, Dash flung himself around the pole, catching some air. It was an impressive move, especially for someone who had been at this for less than ten minutes. At least Elliot assumed Dash had been at this for less than ten minutes. With him, there was no telling.

Dash dismounted with a flip, landing solidly on his feet. The whole group looked at him in awe, unsure of what they'd just witnessed.

"How the hell are you so good at this?" Liam asked.

Dash shrugged. "It is easy."

"This is what Twitter didn't catch," Talia joked. "All that quality time with Frisky."

"We agreed never to speak of that," Dash said, pointing a finger at his girlfriend. Talia smiled coyly in return, blowing him a kiss.

"Who's Frisky?" Haven whispered.

"That's the stripper from Vegas," Elliot answered, hoping Haven remembered the story. He didn't want to have to go into details here about Dash's PR nightmare after the

Fremont Cup that had landed him a suspension from the team. It was a wild story, but one that had caused him a lot of anguish along the way. In the end though, he and Talia had ended up together, so there was at least a happy ending.

Haven nodded in understanding, turning her attention back to the pole, trying to mimic what Dash had just done. She had all the grace of a foal trying to find its footing, but it didn't matter. The pure joy that was wafting off her was enough to power the whole city of Atlanta. The juxtaposition of her shimmying down a stripper pole while wearing a T-shirt that read "I was raised on the street," featuring a picture of Big Bird, Ernie, Bert, and Oscar the Grouch, however, was more than enough to fuel all his own dirty fantasies. There was nothing about her that didn't get him going, that didn't excite him. Who cared if all the other teachers thought she was a Goody Two-Shoes. That's how he liked her. That's what made her Haven.

"What's that smile for?" she asked, twirling, one hand grasping onto the pole, the other held out wide.

"I'm not sure that this activity is Big Bird approved." Elliot nodded at her shirt. "Hi kids, the letter of the day is S, for stripper."

"It's E, for exercise," she countered.

"Well played."

"And I love this shirt. I'm a little bummed that Elmo isn't on it, although I do understand the choice to exclude him, given his current celebrity status, and the fact that he's not an OG *Sesame Street* character. But, I do love the little guy."

And I love you...

"I know. I remember the stuffie you carried around for forever. You tried to take it with you to school."

"Hudson had to sit me down and explain to me that wasn't something the big kids did. Like you guys were really 'big kids' at eight," she remembered with a laugh.

Hudson.

His best friend's name hit him like a wrecking ball. The best friend who was going to have Elliot's balls if he ever found out about all the things Elliot had done to his baby sister. A pang of guilt sliced through him, eyes still glued to the adorable brunette in front of him. Hudson had been one of his first thoughts when Haven brought up her whole naughty-list scheme. Yet, he had barely crossed Elliot's mind since. Great friend he was.

"I have a couple of kiddos in my class this year that bring their stuffies with them," Haven continued, pulling him back into the moment. Squatting down, she twerked for a second, before slowly standing back up, running her hand along the backside of her leg and over her perfect ass. Fuck, was she sexy. Forget Hudson. Elliot could deal with how he was going to handle his best friend later. Right now, focusing on Haven was all that mattered. "They have to stay in their bags, but I think it helps them to know they are close. And if we have a moment that's too much, they can go give them a squeeze."

"What if I want to give you a squeeze?"

Haven stopped her movements, the sparkle in her eyes turning to something else. Something much naughtier.

"Depends on what you planned on squeezing."

Stepping into her, their bodies flush against one another, he placed his hand squarely on her ass. Just tight enough to claim it, but not quite a squeeze. Yet.

"I thought I'd start here, then maybe work my way around to the front…"

Haven's breath hitched, a small squeak escaping. He was onto something.

"Then—"

Bang!

A loud thud stole their attention, Avery's high-pitched

laughter cutting through the air right behind it. The happy sound was muffled by Liam's deep timbre muttering a string of Irish curses.

"If you just fell on your ass and I missed it, I'm gonna be pissed," Talia said.

"Don't worry; I'm pretty sure I got a video!" Delaney called out.

"I wanna see!" Avery said, as she tried to catch her breath.

Haven broke away from his hold, rushing over to the girls to watch whatever Delaney had caught on her phone. As sad as he was that their moment was interrupted, he couldn't blame her. The video was likely to be one they laughed at for a long time. He also couldn't help but enjoy watching how well she fit in with this group, how easy it all was. Maybe that piece of this didn't have to be temporary.

A few hours later, after finishing up with Jazzmin and grabbing a bite to eat at a pub a few blocks over, the group said their goodbyes. Liam and Avery were off to Ireland in a few hours, while Chance and Delaney were flying home to Denver tomorrow afternoon. Dash and Talia were staying in town, since everyone—including both Talia's extended family from Arizona and Dash's mom and sister from Argentina—was coming here. Lots of hugs and promises of texts later, Elliot and Haven were finally back in the car on their way to his place.

"I know it's not Christmas Eve yet, but since you're staying at my place tonight, I was thinking we could watch *Chasing Snowflakes* if you wanted tonight," he said, eagerly awaiting her answer. It was her own personal tradition to watch the Hollie Berry movie every year, reciting the dialogue right along with the actress.

"Hot cocoa and all?"

"I even have the jumbo marshmallows."

"Squeee! OMG, Dobby, you are seriously the best! I could kiss you!"

"I won't say no to that."

"You're driving," she pointed out. "It's unsafe. So it will have to wait until we're parked. And then maybe…also…"

Elliot glanced over at her, and her sudden nervousness was palpable.

"Then, maybe…also…what?" he prompted.

"I was just thinking that maybe after the movie, but before sleepy time, that we could have an encore of last night?"

Fuck yes…

"An encore, huh?" he teased. "Well, Miss Haven, I dunno. We already checked that item off your list."

"I know, but there isn't a rule against checking it twice."

Checking it twice. He liked that.

"Then I'll give you as many encores as you'd like."

CHAPTER ELEVEN

HAVEN RAN her fingers through her hair, in a last-ditch effort to make herself look presentable. Finger combing never seemed to work all that well, but in this moment, in the airport bathroom surrounded by what felt like a bajllion people all trying to get somewhere for the holidays, it would have to do. It wasn't like Hudson would comment anyway. He didn't pay that close attention to her. And even if he did, she could just blame the chaos of traveling. No need to mention the part about his best friend bestowing a life-altering orgasm upon her at ten thousand feet, courtesy of vibrating panties.

And damn, was it an orgasm to remember.

Sighing, she gave herself one last glance in the mirror, wishing that the ache in her chest would go away. It had appeared almost as soon as the plane had landed, wheels skittering across the tarmac. She should be excited to be at home, to see her family, when in reality, she felt like Pigpen from the *Peanuts* cartoon. Only instead of a cloud of dirt surrounding her, it was dread.

With one last heavy exhale, Haven shrugged on her coat, covering up Elliot's jersey. She'd felt a zing putting it on this morning, excited to show it off to him. She wore it to every game, but today was different. Today she wasn't wearing it as his little sister—but as his girl. Elliot's eyes all but popped out of his head when she'd walked out of the bathroom in just his jersey this morning, his hard, punishing kisses almost making them late for their flight.

"Well, that's that then," she muttered to her reflection, trying to force a smile.

Those had been Elliot's words as they taxied to their gate. The magic words that had sucked all the joy right out of her. Was this what it was like to experience the Dementor's kiss? If so, no wonder chocolate was required to recover. It was certainly going to be a staple in her life over the next few days.

Of course it's over; you completed your list...

It was true, she'd checked off everything on her naughty list. The only exception being 'take a naughty photo.' But she'd added the pole dancing last minute, so it felt like a wash. In her mind, she could picture the list, written out in a pretty, looping font, a glittery red ink on an old-fashioned scroll, just like the one Santa was always depicted as holding, little check marks next to each item. Two marks next to the biggest item of all—a one-night stand.

No, that wasn't right. There were two items they had checked off twice. A one-night stand and fooling around in public. The latter one she'd never intended to accomplish this weekend. It had an R next to it on the original list. A relationship item.

Suck it up, Buttercup...this wasn't a relationship; this isn't a breakup. He was just lending you a helping hand...and the best sex of your life...

"What's the matter?" Elliot asked, pushing off the wall he was leaning on outside the women's room. "You went in there smiling, then you came out looking like someone just told you Santa isn't real."

"Shhhh!" she scolded, furiously looking around to make sure that there weren't little ears that could hear. "Santa is very real, Daubney Blake. And don't you forget that!"

"Sorry, sorry. But really, what's going on?"

Shit. Shit, shit, shit...

"I'm just tired," she lied. What else could she say? Thanks for all the orgasms? Oh, and these last three days have made me realize that I love you and that I want to be the mother of your children? Kthanksbye! No, absolutely not. "Some guy kept me up all night, plying me with hot cocoa and my favorite Christmas movies."

And some seriously epic sex...

"I see."

Elliot nodded, not saying another word, simply slipping his hand around hers as they made their way to baggage claim. It was a move that seemed so natural and easy, as if they did it every day. Like Haven's insides weren't simultaneously melting and doing a Christmas jig from his touch. Would it really be too much to ask of the universe for this to be the rest of her life?

"Hold up," Elliot said, stopping right before the exit out of the secure area and into baggage claim. Haven looked up at him, heart slamming against her rib cage. Every millisecond that passed felt like an eternity with Elliot's soulful eyes staring back at her. "One more for the road?"

One more—

Her thoughts were cut short by his mouth locking on to hers, stealing a kiss. Haven's mind went blank, her whole body leaning into him. He kissed her like she was the last woman on earth, and she returned the efforts in kind. If this was going to be the last one of these she ever got from him, she was damn sure going to make it a good one. A memory that she could hold on to for the rest of her life, so when she was old and gray, thinking back on the one that got away, she would still be able to feel this in all the ways she was feeling it now.

Elliot pulled back slowly, adding in a couple of quick pecks, like he too was committing it to memory. Every fiber of her being was screaming to tell him she wanted more. That she wanted him. All of him. But she couldn't. She was being relegated back to being nothing more than the best friend's little sister.

A blink of an eye later, Elliot took her hand again, leading her through the crowd. A loud crash sounded behind them, Haven unsure if there had been an accident of some kind or if that was just the sound of her heart shattering. Really, it could go either way.

"Hey, you two!" Hudson called, waving frantically at them, stealing her attention from whatever was going on behind them. Their bags were propped up next to him, all ready and waiting. Elliot dropped her hand as soon as Hudson was in sight, the sudden lack of warmth making the loss of his touch even harsher. "Took you long enough to get out here. Not often the luggage beats you."

"I had to pee," she answered, knowing he'd buy the excuse. *And remove the vibrator your bestie used on me from my panties.* Hudson wrapped his arms around her in a bear hug, squeezing tight. She loved her big brother and was thrilled to see him, but it did little to ease the sting of the unsaid goodbye. "The ladies' room two days before Christmas in an airport is a kind of chaos that I do not have words for."

"I believe that," Hudson replied. Turning to Elliot, he gave him a hug just as monstrous as he had given her. "But let's get in the car and get home. I have got to tell you all about the new project I'm working on."

For the next forty-five minutes, they listened to Hudson prattle on about work, barely coming up for a breath. It was a nice distraction while it lasted, giving her something to think about other than how sad she was. That was, until they pulled into their driveway, making her face the only thing worse than having to be around Elliot knowing he was no longer hers—not being around him at all.

Piling out of the car, she couldn't help but let out a long, ragged breath, taking in the brick Tudor-style house next door, with its elaborate chimney and covered front porch. She'd never thought much about the house, other than it nicely matched the one she grew up in directly in front of her. The driveways mirrored each other, a small patch of grass separating them, making it one of many spots that Elliot and Hudson occupied through their childhood. Elliot's parents still lived there, meaning he wouldn't be far away. Yet, it might as well be a million miles as far as she was concerned.

"Grub Pub tomorrow?" Hudson asked Elliot, closing up the back of the car.

Haven flinched internally at the question, hating that Hudson was making plans with Elliot. That wasn't fair; she knew that. Lunch at Grub Pub, a local bar and grill that was the very definition of a dive bar, was their Christmas Eve tradition. They'd been doing it since they were teenagers and old enough to drive themselves. Nonetheless, she was jealous. She wanted to go on a date with Elliot. To have more time alone with him. Instead, Hudson got to.

"Of course," he nodded. "Well, I better get inside. Mom has already texted me that she has lunch waiting. See ya."

See ya...?!

Haven wasn't sure what she'd been expecting, but it

wasn't that. Then again, his exit there was normal. A week ago she wouldn't have thought twice about it. Now it was enough to make the pieces that her heart was already in shatter a little more.

Relegated indeed.

CHAPTER TWELVE

EVERYTHING ABOUT GRUB PUB was the same. Same décor, same menu, same obscure rock playing too loudly over the speakers. Nothing about this place ever changed. Even the food tasted exactly like it always had.

Yet, something was different.

Something was…off.

The eclectic mix of street signs and pictures from the seventies—all of which had been on the wall since the seventies—should have been comforting. Taking another bite of his burger, Elliot hoped once more that the taste of home would spark something in him, knocking him out of this funk. It wasn't working. The onion rings also hadn't done much. And forget the beer. If anything, he was starting to think that might be making it worse.

Whatever *this* was had settled in him almost the moment the front door to his childhood home had shut. The feeling was instant and oppressive, and hadn't budged one bit since appearing. He'd managed to put on a happy face, not letting either of his parents suspect that he was anything but overjoyed to be at home with them. When his older sisters and their families arrived for dinner, the kids had kept him distracted for a little while, but not long enough. The sullen sensation rose back up in him, his insides feeling like they had been shredded with a million tiny forks. He just wished he knew what this feeling was.

Actually, that was a lie. He knew what this was.

Heartbreak.

He also knew how to fix it. Too bad that wasn't easy. Or possible. Haven had made it perfectly clear that he was a means to an end, and that it all ended when they got back home. For a second when she'd whispered she was wearing *the* panties on the flight yesterday, encouraging him to bust out his phone and see what they could accomplish, he'd thought maybe that she'd changed her mind. That maybe this would continue once the plane landed. He'd even given it one last go with that kiss, praying that she would tell him that she wanted more and that it couldn't be their last kiss. But she didn't. She'd simply accepted it for what it was—a beautiful, final note on an amazing weekend.

"You haven't heard a word I've said, have you?" Hudson asked, kicking him under the table.

Shit...

"Errr, sure I have."

"Yeah? Then what did I just say?"

Fuck. Elliot had no idea. His best friend was right; he hadn't heard a single damn word Hudson had said since they sat down. His head had been too filled with thoughts of Haven—her smile, her laugh, and that cute way she dipped marshmallows into her hot cocoa. Tamping down the urge to ask Hudson how she was, he cleared his throat and owned up to his distraction.

"Sorry, man, head's just not in the game today."

"Hope you're not like this on the pitch, or that career of

yours is over and you're going to have to survive on all that studying you didn't do in college."

Elliot nodded. Thankfully it was the off-season, but if he didn't snap out of this, he was sure to lose his starting spot next season. Surely he'd be over this by that point, right? Then again, he'd been secretly in love with Haven for years. Now that he'd had a taste, he wasn't likely to recover quickly. Or at all.

"It's that girl, isn't it? The one you've had a thing for but won't ever talk about?" Hudson continued. Elliot shrugged in response, unable to give him more than that. Hudson knew there was someone, just not that the someone was Haven. And that was for a reason. If he found out...well, Elliot didn't even want to think about what Hudson would do then. "It's gotta be her. Either that or there is something in the water down there in Atlanta. Haven's done nothing but mope around since you two landed."

"What?"

Hearing her name made his heart skip a beat. He wanted to ask more, get some details, but that would be suspicious.

"I dunno what her problem is, but she changed into her pj's like the second she walked into the door, crashed on the couch, and hasn't moved. Something about coal."

Coal.

Claiming her coal...isn't that what Haven had said she was doing? That was what had prompted her to make the list in the first place. That and the teasing from her coworkers. A pit formed in Elliot's stomach, a realization hitting him. Was Haven regretting their time together? They'd crammed a lot into three days—lots of things that were so un-Haven. He'd thought she'd been enjoying it though, exploring a new side to her. One that even if she didn't ever bust out again, helped her know what she liked and didn't like. Had he known she wasn't into what they were doing, he would have stopped.

Fuck, he hated the idea that she regretted anything that happened between them. Sitting on the couch with her would have made him just as happy as that damn pole-dancing class.

"Hell, if I didn't know any better, I'd think I was dealing with a pair of broken hearts. That the two of you were hung up—" Hudson stopped, French fry hovering just before his mouth, realization dawning on him. The hamster on the wheel in his brain was moving double time. Elliot could see it all being worked out. Fuck, he was in deep, deep shit. Dropping the fry, Hudson finished his sentence, "on each other."

And there it was.

The truth. Out there in the open, for the world to know.

Elliot swallowed hard, waiting for more of a reaction from Hudson. The walls seemed to be closing in, the temperature of the pub rising by the second. Hudson sat perfectly still, but Elliot could feel the tension in his body. He knew his best friend. This was his process. Stillness, followed by one of two things—deep, gut-busting laughter or searing anger. He also knew which one to expect.

"You...you and Haven..."

Nodding slowly, Elliot smiled, memories of her kisses flooding him. There was no use in denying it.

"This girl that you've been hung up on for years, the one you've never made a move on, always saying that you can't, and I quote 'because reasons'...is Haven? My sister, Haven?"

"Yes. And before you say it out loud, yes, you're 'reasons.'"

Leaning back, Hudson erupted into laughter. The loud, uncontrollable kind that comes with friendship as old as you are. It was the exact opposite reaction than what Elliot was expecting. This was Hudson's reaction to them getting into the first choice of college, and when Elliot had been drafted. This was his happy reaction.

"Why the fuck didn't you say anything, man?"

"Excuse you?" Elliot said. He hadn't heard him right. Was…was Hudson okay with this?

"All this time I've been picturing some hot, leggy blonde who was just sex walking. And you've been talking about Haven. 'I have coordinating theme clothing for every season and holiday' Haven. 'I sing both verses of "I'm a Little Teapot" while boiling water' Haven." He continued to laugh.

"I happen to adore both of those things about her," Elliot defended. "Especially the 'I'm a Little Teapot.'"

"Okay, okay," Hudson said, trying to calm his laughter. "So, like…what? Did you finally make your move? You go all Alpha Elliot on her? Wait, ew. Ew, ew, ew, ew, ew. Sister—don't answer that!"

Elliot barked out a laugh of his own. Alpha Elliot. Hudson hadn't called him that in a long time. Hell, probably not since college, when he'd heard Elliot and his then girl-friend through the thin walls of their apartment. The amount of shit Hudson had given him seemed like it would never end. Until he'd heard Hudson try and steal one of his moves. In this moment though, he had no intention of going into any kind of details—it'd been a long time since they'd shared that kind of stuff anyway—but the idea that he could confide in Hudson about this felt good. Damn good.

"Yes, I mean…" He paused, needing to find the right words. "Yes, something changed between us. Or so I thought. I've had feelings for her for a long fucking time, dude. I've just never owned up to them because…"

"Reasons."

"Reasons," Elliot repeated, his body starting to relax. "She needed help with something, so I agreed. One thing led to another and…well, you're a smart guy; use that brain of yours. But I need you to know that this wasn't just me using her. She really does mean a lot to me. Everything. She means everything to me."

There, he'd said it.

"She doesn't call you that stupid house-elf nickname in the sack, does she?" he asked, bursting into laughter again. "Nope, don't answer that! Sister."

"You're really cool with this?"

Elliot couldn't wrap his head around it. He would have bet good money that Hudson would be pissed right now. Although thinking it through, he couldn't figure out *why* Hudson would have been pissed. It wasn't like he was some overprotective goon.

"Of course. D.B., you're my best friend, have been since we were five. You're already like a brother to me. If there is anyone I trust with my actual sister, it's you. You're sure as fuck light years better than that one guy, what was his name…" Hudson snapped his fingers, trying to recall Haven's ex.

"Paul." *Fucking Paul…*

"Yeah, Paul. Hated that fucker. It might take some getting used to, but if she's the one you want, I'm here to support you. As long as you love her and treat her right. Which, considering the state she's in, maybe I should question that."

"I promise, she's the heartbreaker here. She just doesn't know it."

"So, what are we gonna do about it?"

I'm sorry…what?!

"What are *we* going to do about it?" Elliot parroted.

"Yeah," Hudson shrugged. "Told you, I'm here to support you. So tell me what you need to pull off one of those grand movements like in all those damn Hollie Berry movies she likes so much."

"Grand gestures."

"Yeah, that."

Elliot sat up, grabbing an onion ring, taking a large bite. The intense flavor from the pub's secret recipe of spices hit his tongue, bursting in a way he hadn't experienced before. Life had been breathed back into him. Hudson was on board, and it was time to go get his girl. If she'd have him.

"I do have an idea."

CHAPTER THIRTEEN

ROLLING ONTO HER SIDE, Haven glanced at the glowing red numbers on the old clock radio. Six fifteen. Of course.

Any other day and she would be cursing the alarm that was chirping at exactly this moment. But here she was, on Christmas Day, wide awake. She shouldn't be surprised. Yesterday had been the same way. Apparently her body clock was stronger than she had realized. Not that she'd slept well either night, lying in bed awake, wishing that Elliot was next to her.

It was stupid of her, she knew that. She'd asked him for a one-night stand, not a marriage proposal. And to be fair, she'd gotten two nights, so he'd given her double what they'd agreed upon. That didn't stop her from wanting more. From wanting him. She'd lost count the number of times that she'd reached for her phone, thinking about texting him. Every time she'd opened their message thread, her thumbs forgot how to work. Either that, or her brain did.

Exactly what did you say in this situation? She wasn't interested in just sex. And the last thing she wanted was to look like one of those girls—the ones that her brother and

D.B. had always complained about in college—who got overly attached and seemed to be planning a wedding after only a few dates. She just didn't want to feel this raw ache that had been gnawing at her since she watched him walk up his driveway two days ago.

With a heavy sigh, she rolled onto her back, stretching her legs out. It was early, but she might as well get up. It wasn't like she was going to get any more sleep. No one else in the house would be up, so at least she wouldn't have to fight anyone for the remote. There was probably a Hollie Berry movie on, and if anything was going to cheer her up, it was that. Arching her back, she pointed her toes, trying to get more of a stretch, and her foot came into contact with something.

The soft thud of it hitting the floor startled her, making Haven sit upright. It was dark in her room, the sun still asleep with everyone else. Squinting into the darkness, she tried to figure out what could have been on her bed. Her phone was on her nightstand and was much smaller than whatever she'd hit. Curiosity getting the better of her, she flipped on her bedside lamp, crawled to the edge of the bed, and peered over. A rectangular, white shirt box lay on the floor, a simple green ribbon wrapped around it.

What on earth...

Picking it up, she gave it a shake. Something moved inside but didn't make much of a noise. For a second she wondered if it was Christmas pajamas from her mother, but that didn't make sense. She'd stopped the new-pj's-on-Christmas-Eve tradition after she and Hudson had both graduated from college. It was highly unlikely she would be starting up again now.

Haven shook the box again, hoping this time it would give her some kind of clue. Nothing. Pursing her lips, she wondered if it was okay to open it.

It's Christmas and it's on my bed...I'm opening it...

Giving the ribbon a tug, she slid it off, flipping the box open. A typed note lay on top of the tissue paper.

A little something from Santa...

Now she was really curious. Pulling back the sparkly white tissue paper, Haven's eyes went wide, instantly filling with tears. Her pulse started to race, the purple fabric staring back at her. Apparently Santa had known exactly what to get her for Christmas.

Miss Frizzle's solar system dress.

Haven lifted the dress out of the box, holding it up to the light, taking it all in. It wasn't an exact replica—this was sleeveless with a scoop neck instead of the button-up collared version Miss Frizzle had worn in the book, but there was no doubt that this dress was modeled after it. Moons, stars, planets, and all. Swallowing hard, Haven fought back tears. There were only two people who knew how much she wanted this dress.

One was down the hall, probably snoring like a chainsaw. The other was next door.

Unless…

Haven rushed out of her room, thundering down the stairs like an elephant, making enough noise to wake the whole house. She didn't care one bit though, her heart leading the way. She knew it was a long shot—the dress was probably from Hudson, just trying to cheer her up. He'd badgered her all day yesterday about her mood, even agreeing to watch *Chasing Snowflakes* with her, thinking it would fix something. But logic was not winning out in this moment. Hope was. And hope was sending her racing toward the Christmas tree.

"Whoa there, killer."

Haven skidded to a stop, her heart slamming against her rib cage, threatening to break through. Standing before her, backlit from the glow of the tree, was Elliot. He looked too sexy for words in his flannel pants and a long-sleeved Atlanta Rising shirt, hair ruffled like he'd just rolled out of bed. Given the time of day, he probably had.

"Dobby," she whispered, unable to say anything else. Her mind was racing right along with her heart, trying to make sense of it all.

"I love when you call me that."

"W-what?"

Stepping closer, the corner of his mouth quirked upward into a smirk. "I love that nickname. I mean, I don't plan on letting the guys call me that, but from you, it makes my heart swell. Just like I love your snowman dress, and the Sesame Street T-shirt, and that crazy little leprechaun outfit you bust out every March. And I especially love that dress with the crayons on it. It makes me look forward to the first day of school every year."

"Really?"

"Really. I love that I know the second verse of "I'm a Little Teapot" because of you. I love that you give zero shits about using kid-safe words at all times, even in regular adult conversation, because you care enough about your kids that you don't want to slip up around them. I love that to you, the first grade might as well be the wild, wild west, which pretty much makes you Annie Oakley."

Haven huffed out a laugh, tears welling in her eyes. She was losing the fight to keep them from falling. Was this really happening? It was like a scene from a movie, and at any moment she was going to wake up.

Elliot took another step forward, his hands landing on her hips. The weight of them there was one of the most comforting things she'd ever felt. Like they had been sculpted to fit perfectly in that spot. Heat radiated off him, the smell of him filling her nostrils. This was definitely real.

"Dobby…I…" she started, trying to find her words. A tear escaped, rolling down her cheek. Elliot caught it with his thumb, wiping it away.

"Am I being unclear, or do you just not know what to say?" he asked, smirking again.

"Yes."

"Then let me put it this way, the clearest way I know how. I love you, Haven. All of you. Every inch of the silly, sweet, fun-loving girl that I have known since she first toddled into my playdate with her older brother. I don't care about what anyone else thinks of you. I think you're perfect."

Perfect.

Haven let out a sob, tears flowing in earnest now, unable to hold back. Elliot loved her.

"The dress. It's…amazing…"

The dress? You went with the dress?

Mentally kicking herself, Haven tried to recover. That was not the right response when the man you wanted for forever told you he loved you. But Elliot beat her to it.

"I know you've been wanting to add it to your collection."

"Dobby, it's incredible. Just like you." Wrapping her fingers in his shirt, she tried to pull him closer. "I love you too. I've been wanting to tell you, but didn't know how. And when you kissed me at the airport like you were saying goodbye, I just wanted to die."

"I kissed you like that because I thought it was goodbye, that you were done with me. And I wanted to die inside. So I needed that kiss to get me through the rest of time without you."

"I don't want to go through the rest of time without you."

"Good, because I don't want that either."

Warmth rose inside Haven, her whole body starting to

tingle. Elliot loved her. The *real* her. She couldn't think of anything better. Rising to her tiptoes, she tilted her head, wanting to kiss him. But Elliot held his stance, eyes flicking upward. She followed his gaze, landing on a sprig of mistletoe, hanging from a clear fishing line, still attached to the rod. She giggled, so happy she could burst.

"I figured it was time for a new list. And since mistletoe kisses had an R next to them, I figured it was the best place to start."

Haven nodded, holding back her correction. They had technically already started the R items, but she didn't want to ruin the moment. That tidbit could come later.

"I love that. Just like I love you," she returned, pushing up on her toes again. Elliot tightened his grip on her, his lips softly caressing hers. Fireworks exploded inside, her knees going weak. Everything was suddenly right with the world, all her worries melting away. Except... "Wait. What about Hudson? OMG, he's gonna have a cow!"

Elliot laughed. "Actually—"

"He's holding the damn mistletoe," Hudson's voice grumbled. "So fucking hurry it up, would you? My arms are starting to hurt."

Breaking away from Elliot, Haven peered around the tree. Sure enough, kneeling behind it was her big brother, holding the fishing rod so the mistletoe rested above her and Elliot. She tried, and failed, to hold back her laughter. He looked so damn uncomfortable crouched down like that.

"Just a few more minutes. Kissing under the mistletoe isn't complete yet. Then we can move on to living happily ever after."

"Now that's an item I want to check twice."

EPILOGUE

One Year Later

"Just how many Christmas cookies did you have at the school party today?" Elliot asked, holding in a laugh.

Haven bit her lip, squinting as she thought about the answer, still dancing across the living room, the large, stuffed golden star sewn in place on top of the hood on her Christmas tree onesie bobbing along with her movements. If he hadn't known any better, he'd have thought she was drunk. But the only thing Haven was drunk on was her love of all things Christmas and maybe too many Christmas cookies. Shaking his head, Elliot crashed down on the couch, drinking her in as she continued to sway to whatever song was in her head.

"Quite a few," she answered, bending over and shaking her backside at him. He gave it a swat, earning him a giggle. Haven spun around, freezing almost immediately, mouth agape, gesturing wildly at him. "Where are your pj's?"

"These are my pj's." Glancing down, he took stock of his

faded black sweats and raggedy old T-shirt. There was a large hole in the armpit, and he knew it was probably time to retire it, but he couldn't bring himself to. It was the shirt Haven had given him when she decided on what college she was going to attend, so that he "wouldn't forget where she was." As if he could have.

"That's not the one I bought for you for movie night."

"You're right; it's not. And I won't be putting that one on."

"Why not?" She pouted.

His hands ached to reach for her, pull her into his lap, and kiss the fuck out of her. Whatever was going to make her smile again. But he held back. He had a point to make. And a plan. Even if that meant an unhappy Christmas tree, currently backlit by their very brightly lit actual tree. Haven had gone more than a little overboard in decorating their apartment. From the insane amount of snowmen on every surface, to the massive portrait of Santa that she'd found somewhere, it was like the holiday had thrown up in here. But Elliot had zero complaints. As long as she was in it, he didn't care how she decorated.

"I draw the line at onesies, Haven."

"But you were okay being the notebook paper at Halloween!"

"Yup."

She was correct. He'd been more than okay being the notebook paper that paired with her pencil costume when they had dressed up for the trunk or treat with Southland Holdings, the parent company for the Atlanta Rising. It had been an easy costume, just a plain white shirt and pants with blue stripes across them. As far as he was concerned, he'd gotten off easy in the couple costume department. Chance and Delaney had gone as Westley and Buttercup from *The Princess Bride*, while Talia had made Dash dress up as a pickle. Paired with her decked out as a deer, it made them a "dill doe,"—a joke her father, their coach, hadn't found quite as amusing as she had. Mahoney and Trent played it cool, Mahoney taking on the role of Hansel to Trent's Derek Zoolander. Liam and Avery had gone all out though, dressing up as Captain America and Peggy Carter. The night had been a blast, but it still wasn't enough to get him to wear a green onesie that made him look like Buddy the Elf.

"But—"

"Haven, don't make me quote Meatloaf."

Face turning serious, Haven broke out into song, changing the lyrics to fit the moment. "But I won't wear a onesie!"

"Pretty much. Now, are you going to come watch *Kissing Christmas?*"

"Yes!"

Jumping on the couch, Haven snuggled up against him, resting her head on his shoulder. She'd been counting down the days, even going as far as making a paper chain like she did in her classroom, waiting for the release of this movie. It was Hollie Berry's first movie since her *claim your coal* moment last year, a new network having picked her up. Haven had squealed so loud when she'd read the news over the summer, Elliot had thought something was wrong. Nope, just Hollie Berry.

"I won't lie; I feel a little bad about cheating on *Chasing Snowflakes,*" Haven commented.

"Are you really cheating though? That's your Christmas Eve movie, so you still have a couple of days."

"True, and we do plan on watch— Hey, why is my stocking crooked?"

"What?" he asked, playing dumb.

Excitement coursed through him, thankful she finally noticed. It had taken longer than he'd anticipated, and he was starting to wonder if he was going to have to call attention to it. His plan wasn't going to work as well if it didn't seem natural.

"My stocking," she repeated, pointing to the mantel over the gas fireplace. "It's all wonky."

"You must have hit it when you were dancing."

"I don't think so." Popping up off the couch, she walked over to it, brows furrowed. Straightening it, she paused, tilting her head to the side.

Here we go...

"There's something in here."

"Coal?" he offered, sliding off the couch and into place.

"No, a piece of paper."

Haven turned halfway to him, pausing as she revealed the item. Elliot's heart jackhammered, his eyes glued to her as she pulled out the fancy piece of "natural" paper he'd picked out at the stationery shop. He'd spent over an hour looking at samples, wanting to make sure it was perfect. Just like she was.

"It's...a list."

"What kind of list? What's on it?"

"A 'life list,'" she read. "Get married, buy a house, raise children, laugh, love, laugh some more, see the world, grow old together. But first, we need to..."

Haven gasped, hand flying over her mouth as she turned the rest of the way to him. Elliot was ready and waiting for her, already down on one knee. This was it. The moment he'd been waiting for—dreaming of—for what felt like forever.

"But first we need to get engaged," he said, finishing the last line on the list. "Haven Mae Taylor, I love you. I have loved you, in some way or another, for most of my life. And I want to spend the rest of my life doing the exact same thing. I want to look in the stands and know exactly where you are when I'm on the pitch. I want to come home to you every night and listen to all your wild adventures in the first grade. I want to hold your hand while you give birth, even if you almost rip mine off in the process. I want to watch you teach our kids their numbers and letters and sing silly songs with them. I want to take you to the happiest place on earth— complete with those silly mouse ears—and witness all the magic and excitement through you. Then I want to take you back to the hotel and have my way with you while you're still wearing those ears—creating our own magic. I want to fill your days with laughter and your nights with the naughtiest things we can think of. Most of all, I hope you want all this too."

"I do," she answered, head nodding furiously, a single tear trickling down her cheek.

Elliot could see the sparkle in her eyes, the smile tugging at the corner of her lips. He felt like he could burst, all of him in love with all of her. Reaching into his pocket, he pulled out the little box, flipping it open. A strangled noise escaped from Haven, something between a gasp and a sob, tears flowing freely now as she stared at the oval-shaped solitaire.

"Marry me?"

"Yes!"

Launching herself at him, Haven wrapped her arms around his neck, knocking him over. He hit the couch with a thud, thankful it didn't hit back. Haven's lips met his, hard and fast, kissing him deeper than she ever had. It was the first of many forever kisses, he was sure. And he couldn't wait.

"I love you, naughty girl."

"I love you too. And if you want naughty, you should see what I'm wearing under this onesie. Or should I say, *not* wearing…"

Elliot groaned, unable to hold back.

"What about the movie?"

"It can wait. I have some items I need to check off a list. Twice."

Want to know just what happened between Haven and Elliot
on the flight home?
Grab the deleted scene by visiting
Https://geni.us/CITDeletedScene

ALSO BY CLAIRE HASTINGS

Indigo Royal Resort

The Way You Make Me Feel

Can't Fight This Feeling

Caught Up In You

What I Like About You

Atlanta Rising Football Club

Out Of Bounds

Pressure Point

Offsides

Assist

Penalty Kick

Slide Tackle

World of True North

Cakewalk

Stand Alone Novellas

A Novel Seduction

I Think We're Alone Now

Hot Mess Christmas Express

Checking It Twice

ACKNOWLEDGMENTS

This was the last book Denali and I wrote together. I don't know if I would have done anything differently if I had known it was the last one he'd be by my side for - but I do know that I miss him every time my fingers hit the keys. I hope y'all enjoyed this story as much as he enjoyed napping while I slaved away :)

Amy - for being my right hand, my Girl Friday, and the better half of my brain.

Kelly - for jumping on #teamclaire and not backing down.

A&B - for everything, always.

KKSB - S is for sisters…and salty bitches. And you four are the best of the best.

To the other Naughty List Authors - this was fun! Thanks for putting up with me.

Lisa - thank you for always answering the phone, even when you know crazy is on the other end. Love you.

As always, Drew and Denali (posthumously), for their unending, unwavering, unequivocal support in *everything*. Thank you for loving my particular brand of crazy. *Ik hou van jou*

ABOUT THE AUTHOR

USA TODAY Best Selling Author Claire Hastings is a walking, talking awkward moment. She loves Diet Coke, gummi bears, the beach, and books (obvs). When not reading she can usually be found hanging with friends at a soccer match or grabbing food (although she probably still has a book in her purse). She and her husband live in Atlanta.

She can be found here:

Instagram | Facebook | GoodReads | BookBub

You can sign up for her newsletter at
www.clairehastingsauthor.com

Made in the USA
Middletown, DE
15 September 2023

38291557R00076